THE FLIGHT OF THE AURORA

AN AUGMENT SAGA NOVELLA

ALAN K. DELL

Copyright © 2022 Alan K. Dell

The right of Alan K. Dell to be identified as the author of this book has been asserted by him in accordance with the Copyright, Designs and Patents Act 1998.

All rights reserved. No part of this book may be reproduced or transmitted in any form or by any means, electronic or mechanical, including photocopying, recording or by an information storage and retrieval system, without permission in writing from the publisher, except by a reviewer, who may quote brief passages in a review.

No part of this book has been aided or generated by the addition or use of artificial intelligence either in the writing of the text, or in the design of the cover.

ACKNOWLEDGEMENTS

JUST OVER ONE YEAR on from publishing my first book in the Augment Saga, *The Re-Emergence*, I'm back again with a third! I can't quite believe it. I owe so much to all the wonderful people who have encouraged me through this writing journey.

The first heartfelt thanks goes to my wife, Emma, who has been such an amazing support to me, offering to alpha-read and proofread, patiently listening while I ramble on constantly, and helping me out with some logical inconsistencies that arose early on in the writing of this story.

Then to the rest of my family who have championed my writing, made cakes and models of Seventeen and so much more: Thank you, you've made it all feel very special indeed.

To my beta-readers: the stalwart Adam Sadler who has had to sit through three of these things (yet for some reason seems to relish the opportunity, the absolute madman) and Gary J. Mack, author of *Impossible Fruit* and *The Secret Magpie*. Your feedback was invaluable and encouraging, so thank you for reading through this novella and for all your comments, thoughts, suggestions and critiques. They've all come together to make a much better book than what I started out with.

I feel it's also important to note that this novella was originally part of an early draft of *From the Grave of the Gods* before I was sagely advised to cut it into separate books. So, I cannot possibly go by without also thanking the man responsible: Mr Drew Wagar, author of *The Shadeward Saga*; the official novelisations of *The Lords of Midnight* and *Doomdark's Revenge*; and of the Elite: Dangerous novels, *Reclamation* and *Premonition*. It was hard work, but absolutely worth it.

I've also managed to find myself part of a wonderful online community of writers both on Twitter and Drew's Discord channel, without whom I would almost certainly have given up on this project by now.

Finally to you, my dear readers: Thank you for buying, reading, and reviewing my books whether positively or negatively. You're why I do this. May this novella spark in you a sense of wonder and adventure as we dive head-first into the future.

CHAPTER ONE
EARLY RETIREMENT
14th August 2043

THE PHONE RANG in the early hours of Friday morning. It was not yet dawn. Roused by the synthesised ringing, James scrambled out of bed amid the darkness and kicked his shin on the bedpost.

Eating his fist to stifle his yelp of pain, he glanced back and peered through the gloom to where Angela lay still, facing away from him.

James sighed quietly in relief as neither the noise of the phone nor his stumbling had caused her to stir. Her hair—normally flame-red, streaked with white—poked out from the covers, its vibrancy faded to a uniform grey in the shadow of the night.

James threw on his thin blue dressing gown and hopped down the creaky stairs as lightly as he could towards the front door, supporting himself on the bannister. The phone rang-off as he grabbed the handset from its cradle and he let out the quietest of groans.

Who the hell could be ringing at this hour? It's three o'clock in the bloody morning!

He squinted at the backlit screen. It was far too bright for his tired eyes, even on the lowest setting. Wiping his sleep away, he yawned then browsed through the call history as he shuffled into his slippers and plodded through into the living room.

On the arm of the sofa was last night's dinner plate. They'd had a Full-English for their evening meal and he'd left a piece of toast half-eaten. Scooping up the slice, he sat down and took a bite, still looking at the call-log on the handset.

I don't recognise the number.

The phone rang once again, taking him by such surprise that he fumbled the handset. It was a video-call. He pointed it at the TV on the wall and answered.

The image of a man flickered onto the screen, slightly distorted by the wide-angle view which made his nose and chin look bulbous and his eyes beady. His skin was a rich brown with cool undertones. A military man in his fifties, he had crew-cut hair and wore a camo jacket, and looked like he was having trouble working the device on his end.

'Hello? Commander Fowler? Oh damn this thing…' The man leaned in close and enunciated loudly, prompting James to lower the volume. 'I am looking for Commander James Fowler.'

James rolled his eyes. 'Who wants to know? Military?'

The line crackled and the image flickered.

'Sorry, mate, you'll have to speak up, I'm wearing my dressing gown.'

'Apologies, Commander,' said the man as the view

returned to normal. 'My name is Lieutenant Colonel Robert Dryden. I'm the deputy assistant director of the International Space Administration.'

'Ah, the ISA,' said James, taking another bite of his stale toast as he threw his feet up on the coffee table. 'Heard you guys found life on Enceladus the other week. Who'd have thought we'd have *two* lots of aliens in our own solar system?'

'*Microbial* life, Commander...'

'Oh yes, of course. Anyway, what can I do for you, mate? And do you mind telling me why it's so important it couldn't wait until first fucking light?'

Dryden cleared his throat. 'To put it simply, I'm calling because we have a job available and I have been informed that you are the best person for it. You came very highly recommended, in fact—'

'James?' said a croaky voice from behind. 'What's going on?'

Dryden's eyes darted to the side.

James quickly hid the scrap of toast from view and turned in his seat.

Angela rubbed her eyes as she poked her head around the doorframe.

'I'm so sorry to wake you, Mrs Fowler,' said Dryden. 'I have urgent business with your husband.'

Angela looked with disbelief at James and then back at the screen. 'So urgent it couldn't wait until morning?'

'That's what I said,' said James with a shrug.

Dryden shook his head. 'I'm afraid not, ma'am.'

Angela scowled. 'Don't call me "ma'am"! James, who is this guy?'

'Lieutenant Colonel Dryden from the ISA,'

'Colonel of what, being a condescending prick?' Angela groaned. 'Fuck it, I'm going back to bed,' she said, before disappearing and storming up the stairs.

James smiled as he watched the empty doorway, listening to the sound of Angela's heavy-footed irritation receding into silence.

'And don't think I didn't see you eating that toast!' Angela called from upstairs.

James's face fell and his cheeks flushed. He turned his attention back to Dryden, who looked like a deer caught in the headlights.

'Wonderful first impression you've made,' said James, retrieving the toast and taking another bite. 'But that's a good point. Lieutenant colonel of what, exactly? Don't tell me the ISA has its own rank structure now.'

'Former Royal Marine, actually,' said Dryden, regaining his composure. 'So, this job...'

'Yeah. Look, mate...' James said, throwing his arm across the back of the sofa. 'I reckon you've got your wires crossed. I retired from the ESA eight years ago, and for good reason, too. I don't imagine there'd be anyone looking to recommend me for anything, especially not now I'm fifty-eight!'

'Actually, Commander, the recommendation came from someone in our R&D department who says he knows you.' Dryden scoffed. 'Besides, you don't look a day over forty.'

James's cheeks went hot again. How much did Dryden know? There were few people in the entire world aware of James's condition, one of whom was dead. Barring Angela and his old crew, there were only a handful of others from the former space agencies, which no longer existed.

How much of their research had been passed on to the International Space Administration in the handover? How much was destroyed? Did they know about NASA and the European Space Agency's Project Augment?

I'd better play this safe...

'Knows me? Can't think who that might be. I don't know anyone in the ISA. Like I said, I'm retired and I'd like to enjoy it with a bit of peace and quiet.' James took another bite then waved his toast-filled hand and grabbed the phone to turn off the screen.

'Captain Austin Queen?' said Dryden.

James paused; a piece of the stale toast hung from his mouth as he stared at the screen.

He stammered and the remaining bit of crust fell from his lips. 'Consider my interest piqued, Colonel,' he said, throwing the toast back onto the plate and putting down the handset. 'Tell me more.'

'Good to hear, Commander,' said Dryden. 'To be honest, I thought it would be a much harder sell. What we have for you is the culmination of nearly eighteen years of classified research and development based on the alien technology you and your team recovered from Mars.'

'Stands to reason, if Queen's involved,' said James.

'Captain Queen helped pioneer this research back when the space agencies were separate, and now we finally have a working prototype.'

I think I know where this is going.

James's thoughts flew back to the events of the first mission to Mars on the *Magnum Opus*. Captain Queen had led the landing party to investigate the object that crashed on the surface, which turned out to be the remains of a vast alien warship. It was there humanity discovered it wasn't alone in the universe; where tragedy struck and James's life had changed forever; where he had become immortal. Soon after waking from his coma, Austin had told him about the research into the aliens' technology.

'Okay, so what is it?' asked James.

'Put simply, an experimental spacecraft,' said Dryden. 'A spaceplane containing the world's first faster-than-light engine. Captain Queen was adamant that *you* were to be the test pilot for its inaugural spaceflight.'

James's eyes widened and he muttered, 'He did it. The son-of-a-bitch actually did it.'

'I'm sorry, Commander. I didn't quite catch that?'

'Oh, never mind.'

That was close. Don't want to drop the Captain in it. He wasn't supposed to have told me anything about his work. Can't believe he remembered me after all these years. Haven't seen him since the wedding...

It had been fifteen years since James and Angela's wedding on the beach in Florida, where they had all watched the launch of the second mission to Mars together. Austin had been James's best man, but over the years they had lost contact with one another due to the nature of their respective work. James had spent his time flying back and forth from Cologne for the ESA. Meanwhile, Austin's work at NASA—researching Achelon drive technology using the database they had recovered—was supposed to have been classified. In all that time, James hadn't been back into space; it had been eighteen years since the *Magnum Opus* mission, and much longer since he'd actually piloted anything. Even with Austin's recommendation, why would this new agency agree to have him?

'Tell me, Colonel,' James said with a measure of caution, 'Why is the ISA considering me now? After Mars, the ESA wouldn't let me near a spacecraft again. Some thanks I get for being the first one there! The closest I got was a short stint as communicator for the fourth resupply mission, and that was only after Major Zhu held the *Magnum* hostage to get me.'

Dryden blinked. 'She held up the ship?'

James shrugged and gave a small laugh as he reminisced. 'She wanted to have a catch-up, and she knew no-one else could pilot it. They nearly took it off her for that.'

Dryden's eyes narrowed. 'I see... Well, to be frank, Commander, you're still a risk factor. That's in no doubt, but not only did the Captain vouch for you, we are also keen to rectify the mistakes of the past. We figured that someone with your unique physiology would have a much greater chance of survival on this mission than an ordinary human.'

James leaned back into the sofa with a frown and crossed his arms.

So, they do *know about my condition, and now it works for them, they want me to sign up again. Same shit, different names. Goddammit, if it weren't for Austin...*

'I'll consider it.'

He picked up the handset and pointed it at the screen.

Dryden raised his hand. 'Wait, Commander, I'll need your answer by the end of the da—'

The screen went blank and James threw the handset down next to him with a flump. He leaned his head back and groaned. The groan turned into a yawn and a stretch which took him by surprise. He'd almost forgotten the time. Opening a single bleary eye, he looked at the clock on the wall, still showing the ungodly hour.

Better go back to bed. Who knows, maybe when I wake up this will all just have been one really shit dream.

'I think you should do it,' said Angela cheerfully as she pulled her jeans up the last little way with a hop. 'It's a great opportunity.'

James sat up in bed and gawked at his wife. The morning sun cast its warming rays through the gap in the curtains, illuminating her half-dressed form. She always was a morning person, but this tonal shift was jarring, even for her.

Angela stopped partway through putting on her t-shirt and looked at him. 'What?'

'I wasn't expecting you to be in favour of this. Not after what you said last night. What was it you called Dryden? A "condescending prick"?'

'Oh god, I didn't, did I?'

'Right to his face,' James said with a smile.

A look of horror came across Angela as she finished dressing, causing James to laugh out loud. With a mock scowl, she picked up her pillow from the bed and threw it at him before bursting into her own fit of giggles.

'To be fair,' she said, sitting back down on the bed. 'I was very tired. What kind of idiot calls at that time of the morning?'

James shrugged. 'He was calling from Budapest.'

Angela picked her phone up from the bedside cabinet and unfolded it, then held it close to her face. 'Hey, phone?' There was a quiet ping and the screen lit up. 'How far ahead of England is Budapest?'

Another ping sounded and an electronic voice from the device spoke, 'Budapest, Hungary, is two hours ahead of Universal Standard Time.'

'Five o'clock in the morning, then,' said James.

Angela stood, folded the phone away again and put it in her jeans pocket. 'Still too early.'

'That was pretty standard back when I was in the RAF,' said James.

'Well *I've* never been in the RAF. Anyway, don't change the subject. You should take him up on the offer, if only so we can see Austin again; it's been so long.'

James climbed out of bed and straightened the covers. 'Is that really a good enough reason to get involved with the ISA?'

As he made to leave the room, Angela rushed around the bed and intercepted him. She came in close and ran her cool hands across his bare chest before interlinking them behind his neck.

'No,' she said softly, 'but I think it would be good for you. Don't think I haven't noticed you've been miserable, ever since you left the ESA.'

'I left the ESA with good reas—'

'I know. I know you did, and I supported those reasons. Training the other astronauts wasn't fulfilling you, and neither was consultancy. They were scared you'd lose control of yourself and become a danger to others, blah, blah, blah.'

'Yeah, despite all evidence to the contrary,' said James.

'I know, I know. I don't mean to get into it again, but this retirement hasn't been good for you, and you still haven't really accepted your condition.'

'Yes I have,' said James as a weary look came over him.

'Believe me, I have. I've long come to terms with the prospect of living forever. But sometimes it can be hard, you know?' he brushed his fingers against her white-streaked hair and looked into the piercing blue of her eyes. He kissed her lips and rested his head against hers. 'After all, you're even more beautiful now than when we got married. Meanwhile, I've aged like a Twinkie.'

Angela giggled. 'Shut up, I'm being serious! Besides…' She pulled away and looked him up and down with a wry smile. '… I can't deny there are certain advantages to your perpetual youth.'

'So what's the problem with my retirement?' said James, leaning in for another kiss.

She stepped away suddenly, leaving James hanging. 'You're not doing what you love! You're barely doing anything at all! The ISA are completely different from the old space agencies, they're under direct UN oversight now. It's worth giving it another chance, isn't it? Plus, we know we can trust Austin.'

'That's true…'

'He knows what we went through fifteen years ago better than anyone. I don't think he'd call you in if it wasn't worthwhile.'

James sighed. 'You're right, of course,' he said with a wave of his hand. Despite all the experiments, the blood tests, and the late Dr Hales's research, the ESA had never been fully convinced that the changes made to James's genetic makeup aboard the Achelon warship were benign. They feared a ticking time-bomb, that the elysian enzyme would awaken in him what Dr Hales had called a 'warrior instinct'. It was complete nonsense. The last fifteen years had shown no such tendency within

James; not even when Dr Hales had pushed him to his breaking point.

It was this lack of trust that led James to take his early retirement, but the years had dragged on and he had become weary, bored and grumpy. His stubborn refusal to acknowledge the slow decline of his mental health was due to his determination that he had done the right thing by leaving. Angela had brought it up regularly for at least the last three years, and James had always dismissed her concerns. Perhaps she had finally broken through enough for him to consider it.

'Alright, I'll call him back and accept the job,' said James as he left the room and made his way across the landing to the bathroom.

'Make sure you do it after lunch,' Angela called. 'I've got my livestream this morning, plus I feel like I should be there to apologise to the guy.'

James cleaned his teeth and splashed his face with cold water, then looked at himself in the mirror. There was a tiredness behind his eyes that had nothing to do with a lack of sleep and, despite his physiological agelessness, he looked haggard. His hair and beard still grew, and he'd let them go. The hair on his head was unkempt and longer than he would have liked, and his face sported the kind of scratchy, un-styled beard that made him look as though he had a perpetual hangover, though he could no longer get drunk.

Through the mirror he saw the door swing open behind him and Angela appeared grinning from ear to ear wearing her new black trilby.

'What do you think?' she said, bouncing on the balls of her feet.

It was her new look for her livestreams. In the last few years Angela had amassed a sizeable following talking about writing, poetry and classic literature. It had become her regular Friday morning activity and lasted a good couple of hours, though the first half an hour of chat was never anything to do with the topic she had prepared. Lately she had turned to her viewers to help decide on a new style. She put it to a vote, and they had unanimously decided she needed a hat.

So now she stood before James in the bathroom in her jeans and favourite mauve Byron-quote t-shirt with her new accessory firmly planted atop her head.

Before James could say a word, she held out her palms, in which sat two pin-badges; one, a gold-rimmed raven with 'nevermore' written on its body; and the other a simple quill and inkwell silhouette.

'Which one for the hat?'

After lunch James and Angela sat huddled together on the sofa in the living room. James rolled the phone handset back and forth between his hands as he stared at the blank screen on the wall, listening to Angela's enthusiastic recounting of her stream. The trilby had been a rousing success, uproariously received by the people in the chat, and she positively glowed. Following the stream, she had left it on her computer desk in the room at the far end of the lounge.

James's mind wandered. During Angela's stream time, he had watched the news and it now occupied his thoughts. Guy Furious had publicly denied involvement in the attempted sabotage of the ISA's most recent uncrewed launch to Skyport Space Station. Thankfully no-one had been injured.

The perpetrators claimed to belong to a group of Guy Furious's supporters. Guy—foremost conspiracy theorist, failed politician, and television pundit—was quick to distance himself from the group, but the facts were hard to dispute. Protests against the space programme in Guy's name continued worldwide and had become increasingly militant in the last few years. It was clear the situation had grown beyond Guy's control.

'So are you going to wear the hat for anything else?' said James, half interrupting. He normally enjoyed hearing about Angela's new hobby, but his thoughts had moved through what he had seen on the news, then onto Dryden and the job he was about to accept. His growing anxiety made it difficult to concentrate, and by the time he came back to the conversation at hand, Angela had long moved on from the topic of the hat, and now wore a spurned look.

'Of course not!' she said after a short time. 'I don't want to ruin it. I'll have to get another one for going out. Now, are you going to call Dryden or just juggle the phone all afternoon?'

James huffed, then found the most recent number in the phone and pointed the handset at the screen.

The panel lit up and the call logo appeared, dancing to a soft chime. Less than a minute later, Dryden's face filled the screen.

'Good afternoon Commander, and Mrs Fowler. I'm glad to hear from you. Have you come to a decision?'

'Well first of all,' said Angela, 'I wanted to apologise for my outburst earlier this morning. I was extremely tired—'

Dryden smiled and shook his head while holding up a hand. 'Not to worry Mrs Fowler. Rest assured, I've been called worse.'

James folded his arms. 'I've made my decision, but before I give it to you, I want to make something abundantly clear.'

'And what would that be?' said Dryden, raising an eyebrow.

'That I'm not doing this for you or the ISA. I'm only doing this for Austin. I don't know you from Adam, and I don't trust the ISA as far as I can throw them. If it weren't for Queen, I'd have said no.'

'Noted.'

'Just so you know where we stand,' said James.

'Don't worry about that, Commander,' said Dryden. 'I think I've got the measure of you.'

'Oh?'

'Yes.'

'Good.'

'Quite.'

'Then I'm glad we understand each other,' said James, nodding. He glanced sidelong at Angela, who rolled her eyes and huffed. 'Ah well, I didn't fancy sitting on my arse for all eternity anyway. Now, where exactly am I going for this test flight?'

Dryden smiled. 'Excellent. I want you on the next available flight to Budapest. I'll let Captain Queen explain the details of the mission when you arrive.'

CHAPTER TWO
The Aurora

Early the next morning, James and Angela boarded a passenger aircraft bound for Budapest. James sat in the window seat behind the left wing. Between his seat being kicked from behind by a small child with inattentive parents, and a painfully flatulent older man sitting at the end of the row, the flight was a nightmare. Swirling overpriced alcohol around a flimsy plastic cup, James consoled himself with at least being able to look out of the window to see the expansive European landscape below while Angela fidgeted beside him.

Wide ranges of snow-covered mountains were punctuated by city-filled valleys; swathes of agricultural land were laid out below like a patchwork of emerald; and densely packed urban centres had roads stretching out from them like antennae, reaching toward the next. All merged seamlessly from one into the next as the aircraft tore through the skies at a curious whisper. Even the cabin was quieter owing to the aircraft's new-fangled, silent engines; the usual jet-plane din replaced by the hushed conversations of confused passengers, unsure what to make of the lack of noise.

'I don't like this,' said Angela through gritted teeth.

'What?'

'It's too quiet in here. Aren't you bothered by it at all?'

James shrugged. 'No, I find it fascinating. This is one of those brand new models from Caine-Dynamics with the ion engines. That's why it's so quiet.'

Angela shuddered. 'Give me the comfort of a roaring jet any day. At least they don't make me feel like I'm going to fall out of the sky. I still don't understand how they got these ion engines anyway, aren't they supposed to be rubbish for flying?'

'Another marvel of Achelon technology,' said James. 'I guess they acquired the blueprints after NASA collapsed. Bit shady if you ask me, but I don't think anybody cares.'

'But how do they work?'

James tapped his nose. 'They work *well*.'

At the end of the flight, James and Angela mercifully glided through customs and the couple were soon on their way by taxi to the new R&D Operations Centre of the International Space Administration. It wasn't far, as the centre had been constructed around the east-side of the airport soon after Hungary won the bid. This was where all of the ISA's experimental technology was built and tested before being shipped off to the other space centres around the world. Due to the enigmatic nature of their work, the facility was understated, looking like a natural extension of the airport.

Good thing the taxi driver knows where it is, thought

James as the electric taxi turned a sharp corner and headed along the side of the airport towards a complex of squat buildings.

I'd have totally passed it by. No signs or flags; none of the pomp and circumstance of the old astronaut centre in Cologne.

The taxi pulled up close to the reception entrance and James grabbed their luggage from the boot. Angela paid the driver and the couple set off for the entrance, which was marked by a set of double doors. The only indication that the facility had anything to do with the ISA was a minuscule logo on the glass of each door.

Inside, the spacious foyer was stark, beige and empty. The recessed reception area in the far wall drew the eye. It was small and sleek, as though taken straight from a corporate catalogue. Polished dark-wood wall panels curved up onto the ceiling behind the front desk. A metal ISA logo, fixed central to the wall, gleamed in the sterile glow from the three accent lights above. The desk itself was a simple black and grey oblong of faux marble bereft of personality, and its seats sat vacant.

James frowned and looked this way and that. There was a door either side of the reception desk, and another at each end of the foyer.

As if to underline his thoughts, Angela leaned in close and whispered, 'There's no-one here.'

'I noticed that. Very strange,' said James. 'Maybe there's a bell over there on the desk?'

The two crept forwards, the only sound the rolling of their suitcase wheels on the immaculately shined floor. They had barely crossed the room halfway when the door to the right burst open and Lieutenant Colonel Dryden stepped through, intercepting them.

'Commander, and Mrs Fowler! Excellent. Don't look so surprised, I asked customs to inform me of your arrival,' said Dryden, holding out his hand, his voice hollow as it echoed around the room.

James looked him up and down a moment before shaking his hand. 'Dryden. You're taller than I expected.'

The man smiled and said, 'Well, you know what they say: "the camera sheds ten inches".'

At least he's got a sense of humour. Everyone at the ESA was so dour.

'So where are we going, then?' asked James, returning the smile.

'This way,' said Dryden, gesturing back to the door he had come through. 'The team are eager to get started. I'll have someone take your bags to your room.'

A member of staff appeared from nowhere and relieved James and Angela of their luggage, taking it to a room behind the reception desk.

The trio then walked together in silence through the doorway Dryden had pointed out, and went along a series of drab beige corridors until they came to a halt at a set of metal double doors. The windows were of opaque frosted glass, and a red light shone on the wall above.

'What're we stopping for?' said Angela.

Dryden pointed to the red light. 'We can't go in yet. The red light means they're testing something in there. I'll let them know we're here.'

He stepped up to the intercom panel and pressed the buzzer. The intervening silence seemed to go on forever, but in truth it was only a couple of minutes before the red light turned green. With three loud clangs the door's magnetic locks disengaged, allowing

James, Angela and the lieutenant colonel entry.

Once through to the other side, a man's voice boomed as he chastised his subordinates. Though the words were unintelligible at this distance thanks to the overlapping echo in the enormous room, his tone and drawl were instantly recognisable. James waited until the man had finished shouting at his team, and stepped forwards.

'So this is what you do for a living now? I see why you like it, old man!' he said, cupping his hands around his mouth.

Captain Austin Queen turned on his heel and marched towards the three of them. He had changed dramatically over the years; his former military-cut hair had given way to male-pattern baldness, his tanned peach skin was now darker and blotchy. On his face, he had a scruffy grey beard, and he seemed to have gotten a bit shorter. His physique, however, was still impressive; a sweat-stained, grey t-shirt barely contained his muscular upper body. It all came together to give him the appearance of a swole Santa Claus.

Brandishing a wagging finger, he shouted in his distinctive Arkansas drawl, 'You'd better watch your mouth boy or I'm gonna straight-up beat—'

He stopped in his tracks and blinked his squinting eyes. Then he fished in his pocket and pulled out some thin, gold-rimmed glasses which he shoved onto his face. His mouth fell open and he shuffled towards James and Angela.

'Christ Almighty, it's really you. I knew about your condition of course, but... my god, you really haven't aged a day,' said Austin, his voice trembling as he approached. He held out his hands to touch James's smiling face.

'And you got old, Captain. What's with the Gandalf beard mate?'

Austin began to laugh, followed by James, and the two friends hugged one another tightly. Austin pulled back, beaming from ear to ear, and slapped James on the arm.

'It's good to see you again, man.' Austin looked to Angela as she came in for a hug. 'Hey Angie, it's been a while, huh?'

Angela nodded as they embraced. 'Far too long.'

Austin stepped away and motioned around the room with a smug look about him. 'Eh? What do you think? Pretty sweet ain't it?'

'This place is fantastic,' said James. 'I hear you made some kind of breakthrough.' He lowered his voice to barely above a whisper and continued, 'And in less than twenty years, too.'

Austin blinked at him for a moment and then grinned proudly, his mouth just barely visible under the long mess of beard.

'Well, we did it. We freakin' did it!' He sighed and put his hands on his hips. 'Come with me.'

With the briefest of nods to Dryden, who then moved off to speak with Austin's team, the Captain led James and Angela to the other end of the room, past the smouldering remains of a satellite: a prototype second-generation solar collector, Austin explained, replacements for the current array of orbiters beaming energy back from the sun to test facilities in Arizona.

'Faulty component,' said Austin, gesturing to the strands of smoke working their way towards the ceiling extractors. 'A minor technical hitch. It's actually an order of magnitude more efficient than the couple we've got out there now.'

'So that's what you were yelling about when we got here?' said Angela.

Austin grimaced. 'The thing damn-near exploded. Who wouldn't be upset about that?'

Soon they had reached the far wall. This end of the room housed an enormous metal shutter and a small door in the corner. Austin grabbed the handle and the three of them walked through.

The hangar was dark and draughty, but James could make out some light leaking through at the far end, making it at least twice the size of the room they had just come from. It was cooler, too, and the whistling wind rushed through gaps aplenty. Austin disappeared into the gloom. From the shadows came the clunking of heavy switches being flipped. One by one, strips of lights in the ceiling came on with a thud, illuminating the hangar in stages. The receding terminator line gradually revealed the room's secret.

At about thirty-five meters in length, and standing nine meters tall, the spaceplane was an impressive sight. It resembled a cross between the sleek re-entry craft from the *Magnum Opus* and a turn-of-the-century STS Shuttle. Its frame was dotted all over with inset reaction control thrusters, and in front of the tailfin was an unfamiliar object which Austin pointed out as the only external evidence of their experimental FTL drive, the name of which the Captain mumbled.

Angela and James both gave Austin a quizzical look. 'Say again?' said James.

With his face turning a deep shade of crimson under

his beard, he grumbled something similarly inaudible.

'Nope, still didn't get that,' said Angela with a shrug. 'Come on, Austin, what's the problem?'

'Yeah, this engine has been your whole life for nearly two decades, mate. Not to mention it's one of the greatest technological advancements of all time. I'd have thought you of all people would be shouting it from the rooftops,' said James.

The Captain's face turned to burgundy as he glanced at James and Angela in turn. He grumbled some more, and shuffled his feet, looking fit to burst.

James placed a hand on his shoulder and said, 'Captain, you have nothing to be ashamed of around us. I know we haven't seen you in a long time, but we're your friends. You can share anything with us. Real-talk, rememb—'

'Alright! Alright! It's called the Austinium Drive, for Christ's sake.' Austin howled as he knocked James's hand aside, his voice echoing off the walls of the hangar.

A deafening silence followed. James and Angela blinked at one another.

'Austinium drive?' Angela mouthed.

James gaped at her for a long moment, then his face crumpled into a grin. 'That... is amazing!'

He turned back to Austin and grabbed him by the shoulders. 'They named the drive after you? That's incredible. Congratulations, Captain.'

'You—You're not going to laugh?' Austin said looking perplexed.

James frowned. 'No, why would I? You're a pioneer. You brought back the Achelon database. You led the team that unlocked its secrets, and your work has led directly to this.' James pointed at the spaceplane and regarded it with a newfound wonder. He turned back to Austin and continued, 'If anyone deserves to be immortalised in this project, it's you.'

Angela raised her hand tentatively. 'What is "Austinium", anyway?'

The Captain's face regained its normal colour. A look of relief spread across it and he said, 'It's the name for the type of exotic matter that generates the stable warp field inside the engine. Cass came up with it the first time we made it at White Sands.' He then looked at James, his eyes damp and red. 'Thanks Jimmy. I've spent years enduring smirks and snide comments about it being named after me. I never wanted it, but after Cass left NASA I couldn't bring myself to change it. It means a lot that you didn't laugh.'

James jabbed Austin with his elbow. 'Just goes to prove what a stand-up guy I am.'

'You may joke about it, but it's damn true.'

This time it was James's turn to blush. It had become far more sentimental than he had intended. Clearing his throat, he said, 'Your ship's very impressive, sir. She got a name?'

'Of course! Meet the *IXS-17 Aurora*, the human race's ticket to the stars,' Austin replied, his eyes alight and once again burning with pride.

Angela brushed her hand against the black ceramic tiling on the underside. 'Love the name. The dawn of a new era. You sure you're not a poet, Austin?'

'Hold on a minute,' said James, 'seventeen? What happened to the other sixteen? Is that really how many of these you've tested?'

'Yeah, well... Yes, and no. We've been counting right

from when we started working on the drive. Number one was a warp field interferometer experiment—the one I told you about years ago—and it took us a very long time to go from there to an actual drive unit. In reality, we've only lost four full-size prototypes.' Austin noted James's look of concern and added, 'But don't worry, my man, this one has completed all its atmospheric, orbital and re-entry test-flights, so we know it's all good.'

'So what do you need James for?' said Angela, hand on hip. 'Don't tell me we came all the way out here just so you could show us the ship?'

'Not at all. Jimmy here,' said Austin as he gripped James's arm, 'has the best job of all. I want you to take this sweet little baby bird of mine up into orbit, flick the switch on the FTL drive and blast off for Neptune. Once you're there the team want you to do some science before you loop around and park it back here on the runway.'

'Neptune?' cried James.

'Yeah, it'll be great. And hey, what do you Brits say? You'll be "back in time for tea"?' Austin said putting on a terrible accent.

'That quick, eh?' said James, scratching his beard.

That's years of conventional travel reduced to the span of an afternoon.

'What made you pick Neptune, anyway, of all places?' he asked.

'Well, it turns out not even highly-seasoned astrophysicists and aerospace engineers are immune to making jokes about Uranus, so that was off the table,' said Austin with a chuckle. 'But, just like it, Neptune hasn't had a flyby since the late Eighties. Only close-ups we've got of it are from Voyager 2. So you'll be recording data and snapping photos while you're flying around it... hopefully.'

'And of course, if anything goes wrong, then you're all hoping my condition will allow you to come and retrieve me,' James said.

'Hey I did say you were a rock-solid, tough-as-nails sonuvabitch, didn't I?' Austin put his hands on his hips, sighed and stared at the *Aurora*. 'Yeah we're pretty much hoping you'll have the most chance of surviving a catastrophic failure out there. Better than any of us flimsy mortals anyway. Of course, we really don't want a failure, so you'll need to be on the top of your game; keep your head on a swivel and so on...'

The three stood together staring at the spacecraft in silence. James considered how strange a coincidence it was that the last time they had stood together side-by-side they had been staring up at a spacecraft as well. Many things had changed over the last fifteen years, but this was comfortable, familiar, and reminded James of happier days.

Austin broke the silence, his low voice wavering with the weight of regret. 'Hey, man. I heard what the ESA put you through. I'm sorry I didn't reach out, there was just so much going on at White Sands and I—No, that's no excuse. I could've vouched for you a lot sooner, or at least done something about it. But by the time I got to hear it, you'd already retired. It must've been real tough, huh?'

James looked down at the floor. 'Yeah, well, it was bound to happen. They sanctioned that prick Hales and his experiments right up until they couldn't control him. Why I thought they'd treat me any better after he was gone is anyone's guess.'

With a frown, Austin touched his shoulder. 'Hey, this

ain't on you. And it wasn't fated, it was a damned disgrace; call it what it is, man.'

'Well, I don't blame you either way. Besides…' James reached out to his other side and wrapped his arm around Angela, giving her a smile and a light squeeze. '… I was in good hands.'

'What about you, Austin?' said Angela. 'You ever find anyone?'

Austin scoffed. 'Me? Naw, as I told Jimmy back on the *Magnum*: that life ain't for me. Though I did try a bit of the ol' online dating after Poochie passed. Met a few girls and guys that way, but nothing ever went anywhere. I'm not interested in romance or—god forbid—sex. I was just lonely and all I really wanted was a friend. I'm happier this way, but damn I miss that dog…'

'Wait, what about Cass? I thought you two had a thing going on?' said Angela.

Again Austin laughed, but this time the question seemed to lighten his mood a little. 'I'm sure she'd have loved to hear you say that. She definitely had a thing for me, but she accepted my asexuality and that I didn't want to be involved with anyone. She was a great friend; I miss her a lot. She moved across-country to be as far away from White Sands as possible, and that was that. I stayed, she didn't. No hard feelings.'

James nodded. 'I'm happy for you. But I'm sorry to hear about your dog, mate. I take it you're not ready to get another yet?'

'Not in the slightest! She and I went through a hell of a lot together. Really helped me through some dark times. I'm just glad I was there for her at the end, y'know? Don't think I'll ever be ready for another.

Besides, I'm here most of the time now, so it wouldn't be fair on them.'

Silence fell in the hangar, not uncomfortable but weighty and wistful; a knowing quiet between friends, at once congenial and reassuring.

Austin cleared his throat. 'Anyway... I'd like you to come and meet the people responsible for all this; they're back in the other room.'

James took one last look at the *Aurora* before Austin flipped the switches once again, throwing the spaceplane back into darkness, and the trio returned to the adjoining room to meet Austin's crew.

It was a team of eight, mostly made up of aerospace engineers but also a couple of astrophysicists and a quantum field researcher. The majority of them were standing behind a safety screen talking with Lieutenant Colonel Dryden when Austin, James and Angela approached. The colonel held his arms crossed tight over his chest and his frown intensified the more he listened to whatever the six around him were saying. The remaining two were a few metres away looking over the damaged satellite in the middle of the room. Long, snaking cables connected it to the control panel behind the transparent plastic wall.

'Hey boys and girls, I've got someone special for y'all to meet,' said Austin.

'Captain Queen,' said Dryden. 'Would you care to explain yourself? I have received multiple complaints about your conduct this morning and—'

Austin held up a hand, stopping Dryden in his tracks. 'I know what you're gonna say, *Dad*, but there's no need.'

Dryden huffed and squeezed the bridge of his nose.

'For the love of god, would you stop calling me "Dad". Please, for once, Captain, show a little professionalism. You know full well it's "deputy assistant director".'

'Professionalism? You want to talk to me about professionalism, *Dad*?' Austin said, his face contorting into a scowl. 'Could the Board have shown a little professionalism when they lumped us with this damn solar swarm upgrade at the last minute? What the hell was wrong with Ahmed's team over at the Merkulova Space Centre that we had to pull double duty on these things—' Austin stopped himself and took a deep breath. 'Y'know what? Never mind... I was actually about to apologise to these fine folks for my outburst earlier. So why don't you go back to your little office and I'll deal with this here?'

Dryden huffed again. 'Fine, Queen. But I'd better not get any more complaints.' He glanced at James and Angela, and stepped forward with his hand outstretched. 'Sorry about that, Commander. Once you're finished here, I'll have someone show you to your quarters.'

He shook both James and Angela's hands and marched off towards the door.

When he was gone, one of Austin's team members stepped forwards with her arms crossed. She had light tanned skin, green eyes, and was dressed in a white coverall with the hood up, hiding her hair.

'We're waiting, Captain,' she said in a Hungarian accent, drumming her fingers on her arm as she glared at Austin.

Austin put his hands on his hips and examined the floor. 'Deadlines have got me stressed out,' he said. 'You guys are honestly the best team I've ever worked with, and you don't deserve to be run ragged after making the *Aurora* a reality. They dumped this shit on us and we all know it's just because of the optics.'

'Optics?' said James.

Looking up from the floor, Austin sighed. 'Yeah. Fusion power set a lot of people on edge. I mean, never mind that we practically ended the world energy crisis in the space of about five years with those Achelon designs.' He pointed at the satellite and continued, 'These things are our so-called "safe" alternative. What started as a long-term experiment has apparently turned into The Most Urgent Fuckin' Thing in the World. All because people saw a few memes of mushroom clouds on social media. Anyway,' the Captain turned back to his colleagues, 'I'm sorry for taking it out on you this morning. You're doing great work and we can get through this.'

The team nodded and murmured in approval.

'So, who is this?' said the engineer, fixing her attention on James and Angela. 'You told us our test pilot was of a similar age to you. He is at least twenty years younger.'

'I'm flattered,' James said.

'Uh, good genetics?' Austin stammered, casting a furtive glance to James, which he returned. 'This is Commander James Fowler, and his lovely wife, Angela,' the Captain continued with a gesture in their direction. 'I'm sure you'll recognise the name; Jimmy here was the first of us *Magnum Opus* folk to set foot on Mars. Not only that, this tough-as-nails SOB fought an alien warrior mano-a-mano and lived to tell the tale. He's more than qualified to test our spaceplane.'

'That's nice,' said another of the engineers, an Iranian man with a neatly-trimmed black beard, 'but we need a pilot, not some sci-fi space cowboy.'

James opened his mouth to object, but Angela stepped forwards, cutting him off.

'Oh, he's a pilot, too,' said Angela. 'Twelve years in the RAF. Do you think everyone calls him "the Commander" for fun?'

One of the other Hungarian researchers piped up 'Wait, I thought James Fowler died years ago.'

'Don't bury me just yet,' said James with a laugh, 'I'm only fifty-eight.'

James and Angela chatted with the engineering team for a while longer. They explained the details of how they got the final version of the Austinium drive working, and talked at length about their research.

Some of the younger team members had come on board only in the last few years since the space agencies merged, having taken over from others who had since moved on. They spoke excitedly with James about how important the first Mars mission was to their childhoods and how it influenced their decision to go into aerospace engineering.

The conversation was cut short by a rumbling in James's stomach. He checked the time on his phone: two o'clock. Had they really been talking that long? The only thing he and Angela had eaten all morning was an unbuttered ham sandwich each during their flight. It had stuck to the roof of James's mouth and had all the flavour of a washing-up sponge, so he was grateful when Angela asked one of the engineers to show them to the facility's canteen.

It was more a mess hall than a canteen; a large room

with six long tables set in two rows. At one end there was the foodservice counter displaying hot food in bains-marie under heat lamps. A cheery-looking server stood behind laughing and talking with the staff as he distributed meals of stewed meat and tarhonya pasta, thick vegetable pottage with spicy sausage, stuffed peppers, or simple creamy mashed potatoes and breaded chicken cutlets. Everything looked and smelled delightful, and James quickly scooped up a tray and stood in line, with Angela joining him soon after.

The woman in front of them in the line spotted them and turned to introduce herself. Her eyes were a striking green and her skin a cool bronze.

'Oh, you must be Commander and Mrs Fowler,' she said. Her accent was North American, but James couldn't tell where from; it sounded vaguely southern like Austin's. The woman had long black braids which swung as she held out her hand. 'My name's Ilona, pleased to meet you.'

James shook hers and said, 'Likewise.'

'What do you do here, Ilona?' said Angela, shaking her hand after James.

'I'm one of the flight controllers, which means I'll be in Mission Control monitoring things during the test flight.'

'Really? Well I look forward to working with you, Ilona. I'm sure I'll be in capable hands.' James's stomach growled again and he gestured to the bains-marie. 'What do you recommend?'

Ilona grinned and pointed to the pottage. 'The *főzelék* is particularly good, very traditional and hearty. The chef does a great job with the *schnitzel* too,' she said, giving an appreciative nod to the server, which he returned.

Ilona ordered her food, which ended up being neither

of the two options she'd recommended to James, said goodbye and went to sit down with a group of people James assumed to be Mission Control staff.

'She's hot,' said Angela with a wry smile, leaning close to James as soon as Ilona was out of earshot.

James snorted. 'Can't say I noticed, but now that you mention it, she reminds me of... oh, what was her name?'

'Fiona?'

'That was it, Fiona. I'll never understand why you two broke up.'

Angela rolled her eyes. 'Well if she hadn't dumped me, you and I would never have met. I only started playing D&D at uni because I was miserable after the break-up.'

'Ah, the passions of young love,' James teased.

Angela shrugged. 'I wouldn't call it "love", but she was definitely my first,' she said, playfully jabbing James in the side with her tray.

'Oi, leave it out!'

Angela giggled.

James looked over at the group with Ilona. He'd get a chance to meet them all sooner or later, but for now lunch called to him like a siren, so he turned back to the server and ordered the *főzelék*.

After their hearty lunch, James—whose stomach now gurgled gently with satisfaction—and Angela were shown to their room on the other side of the complex by one of Dryden's subordinates.

James sat on the bed. It was covered in clean-smelling white linens, and he took a moment to test the springiness of the mattress underneath. Angela sprawled behind him and buried her face into one of the pillows.

The room had no windows and could be generously

described as "cosy", but had a lot packed into it, including a mini-bar, TV and a cramped bathroom at the end.

James slouched on the edge of the bed, holding his head in his hands.

Here we are. Me, going back to space. Who'd have thought?

Leaning back, he looked sidelong at Angela, his gaze lingering on her a few moments as she dozed, her breathing shallow and peaceful. She often slept in the afternoon now; it had been only a few years since she'd been diagnosed with type-2 diabetes. It didn't come as a surprise, both of her parents had lived with it, as well as her grandparents and most of her other family members. It was part of the experience of growing older James could never share in; not that he wanted to have to monitor his blood sugar, but it was a sign that the gulf of time between them had begun to widen.

Reaching down and unzipping one of their suitcases, he pulled out a small round device. It was black and shiny, and three little plastic feet clicked out on the underside when he pressed one of the tiny buttons. He stood from the bed and rested the device down on the counter under the television. Sitting on the edge of the bed once again, he leant over and pressed the red button at the top of the curious gizmo.

A door clicked open on the front, revealing an array of cameras. Blue light briefly passed over him from top to bottom, and then again from left to right before a tiny green LED began to blink.

James sat back, rested his hands on his thighs, breathed deep and said, 'Begin recording.'

CHAPTER THREE
Going Public

THE HOLOGRAPHIC RECORDING flickered in lines as the image sat projected into thin-air above the small device from which it was emanating. James's upper body, blurred at the edges, shuffled on the hologram as he considered his next words carefully. Taking a short moment to compose himself, holo-James stared intently at the camera and began to speak.

'Right. Well it's clear I've never used one of these things before. Don't worry, I'm not going to ask you to take over the galaxy like a movie villain or anything. I'm making this recording just in case anything happens to me, and for posterity I guess.

'So, hi Spider, Winston, and all of the two other civilians in the world with clearance to listen to this. You'll be glad to know Angela finally convinced me to get up off my backside and find something to do. Put simply, I'm heading back to space! Great news, right?

I've come to work at the ISA on request from my old CO from the *Magnum*, and it's a great opportunity to be right on the bleeding edge of science and technology.

'I can't talk much about the mission as it's all top secret for the moment. But what I'm involved in is a huge breakthrough, and despite some misgivings, I'm finding myself getting excited for the first time in a good long while. At the very least, it'll keep me busy. You don't need to worry too much. Angela's here and looking out for me as always.

'But here's the thing: If you're watching this, it probably means something terrible has happened and Ange is sitting there showing this recording to you. The mission is dangerous and there are a lot of unknowns. So, I've either died, or become lost in the deep void somewhere. Sounds strange, doesn't it? Reminds me of the words to that old hymn: "Tis mystery all, the immortal dies."

'Just know that this opportunity is something I would have never passed up, and if I have died, then I died doing something I loved. I don't blame anyone. Not you, Angela, Austin, or the ISA. This is one hundred percent something I'm proud to be involved with. Whatever happens, know that I counted the risk and it was worth it.

'Funny, I did one of these messages before leaving on the *Magnum* all those years ago too, but it never did get passed on to anyone even after I fell into that coma. Hopefully this one will actually come out. I mean, hopefully *not*, of course, but you get me. Wow I really should've written a script for this. Anyway, bye.'

The light on top of the holographic projector cut out and the image flickered off. James picked the device up off the table and folded it away.

'Good enough. I'm not doing it a fourth time.'

By the time James had finished recording his message, Angela had awoken from her nap. They had spent time unpacking most of their things, then went back to the mess hall for dinner. Now it was getting late.

Already in her nightdress, Angela watched the recording with James. She knelt behind him on the bed and wrapped her arms around his chest. 'It was lovely. Besides there's a big difference between writing something down and speaking it in front of a camera. Trust me, I know.'

James nodded. 'Speaking of which, you did tell your group there'd be no streams for a while, right?'

'Yes, of course I did,' said Angela. 'Now, what's this about having misgivings?'

James passed the holocam back and forth between his hands. It was deceptively light and he caught himself thinking about the ridiculous amount of reverse-engineered alien technology inside. Such an unassuming device; nothing about it gave a hint that it was anything other than human-built. But here was yet another reminder of the Achelon's legacy, and how pervasive these unwitting benefactors had become to human society.

'The world is changing,' said James. 'It's changing faster and faster with each passing year. Every single new development that comes out of that busted old starship is a leap forward an order of magnitude greater than anything we've achieved in the last century.'

'Well, that's a good thing, right?'

'Maybe. But what if we're going too fast? We barely understand some of the physics involved in any of this stuff. For instance, I couldn't possibly tell you how this holocam works for its size. I can't help but think we'll plunder too far and come undone. That perhaps this faster-than-light engine will actually be the death of me. How do we know it's ready?'

'I understand,' said Angela, 'but have faith in Austin. You know he knows what he's doing. This is his life's work. He wouldn't send you up there if he wasn't sure it was ready.'

James nodded. 'I suppose you're right. I'm just feeling a bit like I'm in the wrong place if I'm honest; like I've embellished my credentials and landed somewhere I've no business being.'

Angela kissed him on the cheek. 'That's normal. It probably means you're in the right place after all.'

James nodded and dropped the holocam back in the suitcase then got himself ready for bed. He climbed between the soft sheets with Angela and rolled onto his side, reaching across her to the bedside lamp. Taking one last look at Angela's infectious smile, he flicked the switch and plunged the room into darkness.

James woke the next morning around half-past six, the excitement of the first day of training preventing him from having a lie-in. He had done the same the day before the launch to rendezvous with the *Magnum Opus*, which had been built in orbit and docked at the International Space Station, and today was filled with that same restless anticipation.

But that's all gone now.

The ISS had been deconstructed nine years ago and allowed to burn up in Earth's atmosphere. The Tiangong Space Station then served as a temporary dock for the *Magnum* until Skyport was built by the ISA at the latter end of 2040.

As he got himself ready in the diminutive bathroom, he leant over the basin and stared at himself in the mirror. Angela was right. Of course he was supposed to be here. If humanity truly was teetering on the edge of destruction, Austin certainly wouldn't be the one to make the final push.

James scoffed.

I'm starting to sound like Guy Furious.

No, if humanity was anywhere, it was at a crossroads. Along one path lay an abyss where all that Guy had prophesied would come to pass, but along the other—along Austin's path—lay endless sky and boundless horizons.

He grabbed some clippers out of his toiletries bag, and with a last wistful stroke of his beard, he moved the buzzing blades to his face.

'You should keep it,' said Angela from behind.

James paused and his gaze flicked up as her face appeared over his shoulder in the mirror.

'Yeah, it makes you look a bit older,' she continued. 'Grow it out some more. You need to keep a low profile about your immortality, even around here. You realise none of Austin's team knows about it, right?'

'No, I... I hadn't.'

'Well, the beard helps.'

Without a further word, James switched off the clippers and laid them down on the countertop.

He and Angela finished getting dressed. James wore his dark green flight suit—the one he had kept since his days in the RAF, which had remained untouched in a wardrobe ever since he had moved in with Angela—and they both headed out of the room into the rest of the base.

They had reached the atrium and strode halfway across in the direction of the mess hall when they were once again intercepted by Lieutenant Colonel Dryden.

'Commander, Mrs Fowler. I trust you had a pleasant night's sleep?' Without waiting for a response, Dryden continued, 'Good. I need you both to come with me.'

'Colonel, we have got to stop meeting like this,' said James, mustering as much sarcasm as he could before breakfast.

Ignoring the snark, Dryden motioned for the two of them to walk with him.

'Can this wait? We're famished and I'm after a bacon butty right now. Don't fancy training on an empty stomach.'

The colonel shook his head. 'I'm afraid not. It's urgent. Walk with me.' Dryden turned on his heel and marched off towards a set of doors next to the vacant reception desk.

James gave Angela a puzzled glance and the two of them jogged a little to catch up.

'So,' said James, 'what's so important that it's coming between an officer and his breakfast?'

'I know Captain Queen promised it would just be a test flight, but,' Dryden took a sharp breath and stopped in his tracks, 'well, the director has other plans.'

'Such as?' Angela said with raised eyebrows and folded arms.

'The director has decided that in light of the Commander's "involvement", he feels the time is right to go public with the *Aurora*.'

James shrugged and leant against the smooth beige wall of the corridor.

'Sounds fine to me. What's that got to do with the price of fish?'

'He's scheduled a press conference for this morning. And, as famous as you are, he would like you in attendance.'

'Famous? Mate, I'm barely a historical footnote. Besides, that's a bit forward; he hasn't even bought me a drink yet.'

Dryden's expression hardened. 'Commander! I'm getting the impression you're not taking this entirely seriously, and it's been that way ever since you arrived.'

'Oi, careful, "Deputy Assistant Director Lieutenant Colonel" whatever,' James spat as he stepped forwards and prodded Dryden in the chest with his finger. 'I'm an immortal guinea pig who's about to be flung halfway across the solar system in the seventeenth iteration of a tin-can piece of shit that looks like it's been designed by a twelve-year-old. I think I'm allowed to be a bit glib.'

James and the Lieutenant Colonel glared at one another for a long moment before the latter broke the silence.

'A... twelve-year-old?'

James's stony expression cracked and both men grinned.

'I'm going to tell the Captain you said that. It's his design,' said Dryden with a chuckle. Wiping his eyes, he looked to Angela, gestured to James and asked, 'Is he always like this?'

After a while, they came to a large room full of ISA staff members and media gophers setting up equipment and a stage, with others rushing to and fro.

Dr Konstantinu Azzopardi—the ISA's first director, and Maltese ambassador to the United Nations—sat at a make-up desk to the far side of the room. He was surrounded by people working on his hair and applying concealer in preparation for the big press conference.

Dr Azzopardi had been appointed as director by the Security Council due to his work at the European Southern Observatory prior to becoming a diplomat. The sharp features of his olive-skinned face were framed by an elegantly trimmed black chinstrap beard and goatee. He held a small pair of rimless glasses in one hand, moving them to his face every so often as he surveyed the jumble of paperwork in his other hand. At the same time, make-up artists worked to spruce him up for the cameras. His manner of dress gave him an appearance more like a suave businessman than the director of a space agency.

As the three of them approached, the director looked up from his papers and dismissed the make-up artists. He stood and, taking a moment to straighten his suit and fold away his glasses, stepped towards them with a smile and outstretched hand.

'Commander Fowler! So nice to finally meet you, I apologise for not doing so when you arrived yesterday. I wanted to thank you for coming in to be Captain Queen's test pilot. And this must be Angela; it is a pleasure.'

Angela gave a slight nod. 'Likewise.'

'Director,' said James, shaking his hand; the director's grip was surprisingly firm and the shake was brisk and confident. 'Forgive me, but isn't all this a little last-minute?'

'Oh, the press conference? Ah, do not worry about it,' the director said with a wave of his hand. 'All you have to do is sit behind me, smile and shake my hand at the right moment. I shall be doing most of the talking.'

Director Azzopardi turned to walk away, but James caught him with another question. 'But, this project has been top-secret for so long, why go public now? No disrespect to Austin, but we don't even know if the drive will work.'

For a short moment there was a dumbstruck look to the director as though James's question was off-script; as though the diplomat-turned-director was more used to being accommodated than questioned.

'Commander—James? May I call you James?'

James nodded and motioned for him to continue.

'Look, I don't need to tell you how important the Austinium drive is for the future of exploration—'

'It's the most important leap forward since the invention of the rocket engine,' said James, his voice tinged with excitement.

'Exactly, so it is only right that the public knows about it. We were being cautious up until now, trying to limit media exposure to the discovery so it did not get blown out of proportion. After all, there has already been so much speculation about the viability of the Alcubierre-White metric over the last fifty years. I have been considering going public with it for a long time; all this inherited secrecy is distasteful to me. But now, with your involvement, this is the perfect opportunity.'

'Looks good for your PR, got it.'

The director gave a polite smile, pulled out his glasses once again and fiddled with them. 'I can see you are not one to suffer pretence. I assure you my intentions are genuine; it is not about looking good for the media, but your name is likely to attract more of the public's attention and hopefully drum up some excitement for the project. A test flight like this should be celebrated.'

'But aren't you concerned about sabotage?' said

Angela. 'This is bound to draw attention from Guy Furious as well.'

'Ah, you are referring to the recent incident with the rocket launch,' said the director, his smile unfaltering. 'If I allowed myself to worry about the detractors of the world, we would not have projects like Skyport, or the Lunar Gateway, or the Far-Side Breccia-Lens Telescope. I take security seriously, of course, but I will not kowtow to bullies.'

'Then it seems I've misjudged you; my apologies,' said James. 'But I hope you don't want us to sit down for makeup.'

'Heavens no!' cried the director. 'I did not want all this myself. All these, uhh, media people want me to "look good" for the cameras.'

James nodded, and his stomach rumbled, reminding him of their breakfast quest. He enquired of the director where they could find some food.

With a smile, Azzopardi pointed to a nearby refreshments cart which consisted of a selection of teas and coffees, fresh fruit juices, a bowl of bananas, apples and oranges, and a variety of fancy biscuits. It wasn't what James had been hoping for, but as he claimed a couple of individually wrapped bourbon creams out of the box, he admitted to himself it was better than nothing.

Three hours passed and the time came for the press conference. James fidgeted in his hard plastic chair which sat at the end of a short row on the small portable stage. To his left sat Captain Queen, then there was a gap to allow visual clearance for the lectern at which Dr Azzopardi stood. The two chairs on the other side of the stage seated the assistant director—whom James had never met—and Lieutenant Colonel Dryden. In front of the stage were rows of seats where the myriad camera crews and journalists of the clamouring press gathered. Angela sat amongst them in the front row, arms folded and somehow ignored.

The whole affair took place outside on a disused runway of the airport, and the *Aurora* had been wheeled out to sit behind the stage, providing the perfect backdrop in the overcast mid-morning light. The stage was lit periodically by flashes from the strobes of photographers in the rows, while tiny drones buzzed this way and that overhead, flying in wide sweeping arcs to the *Aurora* and back.

James tried his best to keep smiling, though Austin made no such effort. On each side of the stage were two free-standing speakers, one high and one low, which were in turn connected to the collection of microphones on the lectern.

With all the journalists present and seated, the clamour died down and the director introduced himself, thanking them for being in attendance on such an auspicious day. He paused for dramatic effect as the strobes went wild, as though giving an ovation in Morse.

'I—*we*—here at the ISA,' he began, 'have a very important and exciting announcement to make. Eighteen years ago our world and our perception of the universe were forever changed. It was then that we discovered we were not alone, and it was not long before we began to reap the rewards of such knowledge. Benefits such as fusion power eliminating our energy concerns; cures for all kinds of diseases that had previously eluded us;

Arcadia Landing, our first permanent Martian settlement, established in 2029; and major expansions in our understanding of astronomy and the physical sciences. So today I am proud to share with you another such innovation: something which I believe represents the single most significant leap forward since the invention of the rocket engine.'

James couldn't help but raise an eyebrow at the director's words, lifted almost wholesale from their conversation mere hours ago.

Azzopardi continued, 'It is our hope that this project will bring about the next generation of space-based propulsion systems and usher in a brand new age of exploration. Our predecessors at NASA and their contemporaries began this important research and we are proud to have brought it to fruition with the hard work and dedication of the world's very brightest minds.' He paused and shuffled his paperwork on the lectern. 'And of course, none of this would have been possible without the help of significant funding from the member states of the United Nations which I, in my capacity as the ambassador for Malta, fought hard to procure.'

The director paused once more.

James scanned the bewildered crowd; the air was electric. Dr Azzopardi was good, a natural orator; he knew how to ramp up the suspense, which kept the assembly hanging on his every word.

'This is something you should all be very excited for, for we have achieved the impossible. If successful, this achievement will open up the stars to us, granting us mastery over the fabric of spacetime itself. You will all be aware of the craft on the runway behind me.' He moved aside and pointed to the spaceplane. 'May I present to you the *IXS-17 Aurora*, the first human vehicle capable of travelling faster than light!'

The director's words met with deafening silence. Eyes darted back and forth on confused faces as the journalists gauged the reactions of their peers. A smattering of overlapping whispers, cutting through the hush, questioned the director's sincerity and sanity. Unfazed, Azzopardi waited smiling, allowing his words to settle. James got the distinct impression he was savouring the unfolding reaction he knew would come.

One nervous-looking young journalist from a popular science editorial raised his hand, holding a stylus aloft. In his other hand he held a small pad, while one of the diminutive drones buzzed above his head like a dragonfly.

'Director?' he asked, his words catching in his throat. 'Are—are you being serious? I mean this has to be a joke, right? Special Relativity tells us nothing can go faster than light.'

Still smiling, Dr Azzopardi moved purposefully, leaning in close to the microphones on the lectern. 'I am being quite serious, Mr Barrett. As for your assertion, *that* is what we aim to determine with our upcoming test-flight.' He stood straight once more and continued, 'I am certain you will all have a great many questions and I will be happy to answer them. However, before we get onto that, I want to take a moment to congratulate those here at the ISA's research division in Budapest who have made all this possible, starting with Captain Austin Queen.'

Austin rose from his seat stiffly and shuffled over to the director. They made a show of shaking hands, and then they stood shoulder-to-shoulder as the director explained the Captain's role in the project. The crowd applauded in a polite, restrained manner that said they were itching to get on with the Q&A.

With the awkward grin and meagre wave of a hermit hauled out of his cave, Austin returned to his seat.

'I would now like to introduce a very special guest indeed,' said the director. 'The First Man on Mars himself, Commander James Fowler.'

There was a sharp intake of breath from the crowd at the mention of James's name. The surprise of the press was to be expected. James had not been in the public eye since the day of the *Magnum Opus* crew's descent to the Red Planet. Like Austin's engineers, many presumed he had died. It didn't help that James hadn't bothered to correct his Wikipedia page which listed his date of death as a mere month after his awakening in the hospital. Still, it was uncomfortable to be stared at no matter how much James had anticipated it.

The eyes of the press bored into him as he rose from his seat and plodded his way to the director with arm outstretched, just as Austin had done.

Keeping a firm grip on James's hand, the director said, 'Commander Fowler has very graciously agreed to come out of retirement in order to be our test-pilot.' Dr Azzopardi then released James's hand and leaned closer to the microphones as he reminded the press of the tragic events of the first Martian expedition.

James's chest tightened and he was back there in the dark of the alien medical bay, trapped in the chamber. Then there was the flash of a blade, the deep void of the Achelon warrior's black eyes, Yula's blood-curdling scream, red dripping from the boots of her spacesuit. The vision changed and shifted; his leg and side ached, and Dr Hales's face appeared, a mess of red, ripped open by a sniper round.

He gripped the side of the lectern, his fingers rubbing the bumps of the wood grain. It was enough for him to close himself off from Dr Azzopardi's words.

The vision began to fade and he fixed his gaze on Angela, who returned his stare with an encouraging smile. 'Focus on me,' the look said. She knew. She'd seen him have these attacks many times over the last fifteen years. She could see the signs, knew his triggers, and she had been his rock. His breathing slowed and the pain receded.

After what felt like mere seconds, James heard a round of applause and came back to reality. He wiped the sweat from his brow and manoeuvred himself back to his seat next to Austin.

'How much longer are we going to have to endure this?' he whispered.

'Just roll with it, man. The director's just winging it himself,' Austin said with a snicker.

James frowned. 'But I saw him reading over his speech earlier...'

'Nah, son. If you'd gotten a good look at those papers he's got on that there lectern, you'd see they're a complete mess. Great mind, excellent speaker, but a terrible planner.'

'So that'll be the real reason we're sitting here at the last bloody minute.'

'Now you're catching on.'

Soon after, the Q&A session began and the questions came in thick and fast from the eager press. Austin answered some of the more detailed ones about the

Aurora's Austinium drive for the science-leaning news outlets, while the director spent most of his time batting away questions about the project's secrecy, insinuations that it was a 'costly vanity project', and arguing the point that there was, actually, room enough for both space exploration and fixing problems here on Earth.

James looked with pity on Dr Azzopardi. He didn't envy him having to engage with these tired debates, and he was thankful that he himself had only to answer a couple of simple questions about life post-coma and why he had decided to come back to the industry.

The director pointed to a journalist who was shorter than the others and almost lost amongst the crowd. Those jostling them quietened and begrudgingly made space for them to ask their question.

'Dr Azzopardi,' they said, shaking their hair out of their eyes, 'there are growing concerns about the gradual rise in fundamentalist doctrine among some alien-worshipping religious groups thanks to what the experts say is "Arcadia Landing's continued interference" with the wreckage on Mars. With this latest discovery yet again making clear use of alien technology, are you not worried that it could be seen as sacrilegious? That the ISA could be tampering with a holy site?'

The director looked taken aback for the briefest of moments, but regained his composure and said, 'I have no such concerns. It was my understanding that these cargo cults believe the aliens gifted their technology to us in the manner of benevolent deities. The notion that our continued exploration of this site could be sacrilegious runs counter to their core doctrines.'

That's not entirely true, thought James. There had been

rumblings that more aggressively charismatic leaders had begun to preach that the research teams on the Red Planet were desecrating a holy relic; that the proper respect must be shown to their Achelon gods. They argued humanity would not be truly ready for the gifts contained within the so-called "Temple" until the proper rites and rituals could be observed. Of course, this would be by way of a priestly pilgrimage. It was an insidious distortion, a way of drumming up more resentment for the ISA while superficially embracing core doctrine.

The alien-worshipping cults were fairly new, the first ones having arisen only ten years ago, but with millions of people thrust into existential crises while trying to make sense of this new reality, they grew quickly. Now there were dozens of distinct groups, each with their own dogmas. Despite their similarities, for now they remained disparate. Still, the authorities watched the cults carefully for any signs of ecumenism. The last thing the ISA needed was a united force of zealots standing against them.

The press conference ended with the director inviting the crowd to return in three months' time to cover the test-flight itself. From there, the reporters and television camera crews spent the rest of the afternoon looking for more detailed interviews from the staff, while Austin led James away to begin training.

The days and weeks turned into months and James clocked in hundreds of hours in the advanced training simulations on the base under Austin's watchful gaze.

Angela wasn't always present; she had been provided a computer and enough equipment to make a decent return to streaming in their small room. But she spent most of her time familiarising herself with the base and its personnel, as well as taking in the sights of the city.

Meanwhile, James brought himself up to speed on all the *Aurora*'s control systems and read huge tomes dedicated to the new drive technology.

After three months on the base, the time came for the test-flight.

It was around six in the evening by the time the flight crews and Mission Control took their places. A breeze blew in from the east which chilled the bones, but otherwise the sky was clear and azure. The low sun cast its long shadows across the runway, the spaceplane basking in its golden light.

James walked out onto the runway towards the *Aurora* amid the buzz of journalists which he ignored. He wore a full spacesuit—sans helmet, which he carried—more streamlined and form-fitting than the one he had used on the *Magnum*, but still coloured in the classic bright white with the ISA's logo stitched to the shoulder. A custom-made mission patch was affixed to the chest, representing the *Aurora* warping spacetime, which James thought was a nice touch.

James shook hands with each of the engineering crew on the runway and ascended the ladder to the cockpit door. He stopped when he saw Austin and Angela running towards him, and stepped back onto the concrete.

'Hey, something the matter, or have you just come to say goodbye?'

'Nope all good, just come to say goodbye,' said Austin, patting a section of the *Aurora*'s wing. 'And to take a last look at my baby here.'

'Well, not to worry mate, I'll take good care of her. Everything's set for launch, and Mission Control's got it covered.'

'I know you will. Just thought I'd let you know I'm gonna be your spacecraft communicator, so I'll be right in your ear the whole time,'

'Damn! And there I thought I'd have a quiet flight,' said James.

Austin snorted and slapped him on the shoulder.

Angela stepped forwards, her hands balled into fists by her sides. He could see the worry in her dampened eyes which glistened in the sun. She'd hidden it well when they had spoken that afternoon before making his final preparations, but it was on full display now. The golden light saturated the red of her hair which ruffled in the wind, but also the way the cold bit her cheeks and the tip of her nose. She wore a hard expression.

'I'll be fine,' said James, putting his gloved hand to her cheek.

She closed her eyes and leaned her head into the glove. 'I know you will, but still...'

James kissed her one last time. 'I love you, and I'll see you in a few hours.'

Angela nodded and stepped back while Austin gripped James's shoulder.

'C'mon man,' he said, 'let's get you up in that ship. Ready to make history... again?'

James nodded and, with one last glance back at Angela, he locked down his helmet and ascended the ladder to the cockpit.

CHAPTER FOUR
ASCENT
15th November 2043

JAMES SAT IN THE SPACIOUS COCKPIT, strapped tightly into the seat at the helm. The panoramic segmented windows gave a clear view of the runway outside. There were lighted buttons, switches and toggles all over the dashboard and on panels above his head. All were within easy reach. There was a small screen almost everywhere James cast his eye, giving nominal readouts for ship systems and even his own vitals. A black flight stick sat between his legs and there was a throttle control fitted to the left side of the chair. It was laid out in a similar manner to the command module of the *Magnum Opus*, except condensed to suit a single occupant. It was exactly like the simulations.

With a sigh he leant his head back against the inside of his helmet. He was ready. Despite it being his first time actually sitting in the ship, he felt as though he knew it inside and out. Under normal circumstances, he would have spent a year in training for the mission, getting himself into peak physical condition, but this time owing to his augmentation, he'd had only three months.

Times had changed. Single-stage-to-orbit spaceplanes were a common sight, mostly as launch vehicles taking astronauts to Skyport. The technology had seen limited use since the mid-2030s but thanks once again to the Achelon, it was now almost fool-proof.

The on-board automations and the variety of screens would help James if he got into too much trouble. This wasn't a test of the vehicle's ability to launch into orbit—that had already been perfected hundreds of times over—the real unknown for which they needed an immortal pilot was the Austinium drive, thus far tested only in sterile laboratory conditions.

As far as Austin and his books had explained, every variable had been accounted for, from the effects of solar wind and the Van Allen radiation belts, to the warp field's interaction with space dust and particulate matter.

The presence of gravity wells—such as those of the other planets—was a concern, and stabilising manoeuvres had taken a significant portion of James's training, but for this mission the route was clear.

Despite all their preparedness, there would always be tiny variances and gaps not accounted for by the prevailing physical theories. Great strides had been taken in understanding the interplay between relativity, quantum mechanics, and gravity—due in no small part to the knowledge contained within the Mars wreckage—but there were still edge-cases where nothing seemed to fit quite right. Like a fishing net holding onto its catch, the success or failure of such a technologically complex drive system depended on its ability to do its job despite the holes.

Laying his concerns aside, James checked the communications system was working and received an affirmative from Mission Control. He flicked some of the switches above his head, activating key electrical systems, then checked aileron and rudder response. Each system reported as nominal as he made his way through the pre-flight checks. The flight stick had a good amount of resistance to it, and with his thumb James noted the position of the toggle to swap over from the atmospheric flight surfaces to the orbital thrusters.

The radio crackled and Austin said, 'Big Bird, you are go for launch. Commence main engine start. Over.'

'Big Bird? That is an awful call-sign, Captain,' said James in mock disgust. 'Utterly atrocious. Over.'

'Well, shit Jimmy, whaddya want me to call you?'

'How about just the name of the ship? Over.'

There was a short pause and Austin said, '*Aurora*, you are go for launch. Commence main engine start. Over.'

James grinned as he flicked a couple of switches. 'Copy that, Hawk's Nest.'

'James, you bas—'

Even using the helmet speakers, Austin's reply was drowned out briefly by the sound of the ship's powerful hybrid engines whirring to life. The spacecraft rattled as James coasted it into position at the end of the runway, and it sat braked, waiting for the countdown.

James looked out on the assembled members of the press waiting eagerly, impatiently, for the historic flight while camera drones buzzed around their heads.

With the engines settled and the spaceplane ready for

take-off, Austin's voice came over the radio once again, '*Aurora*, you're at t-minus thirty seconds. Good luck, and Godspeed.'

James rested his gloved palm on the throttle, ready to push forward. His hands went clammy and one of the screens showed his heart was racing. An eternity passed in the twenty seconds before countdown. All the world watched as James teetered on the precipice of history. Often he had entertained the thought that, as his immortality dawned on him, one day he might blink only to find whole centuries had passed, for time would no longer hold any meaning to him. Now those thoughts seemed a distant fancy as he resided in this moment and felt every excruciating second of it.

Then the announcement came over the speakers inside his helmet, echoed by the runway amplifiers, 'T-minus ten, nine, eight...'

Gripping the stick hard, he eased the throttle open and the low rumble of the engines intensified.

'...Four, three, two, one.'

James disengaged the brake and pushed the throttle control forward a little more. In response, the *Aurora* accelerated rapidly, and James was pushed back into the seat.

The end of the runway loomed close and James pulled back on the flight stick. The *Aurora*'s front end lifted up from the tarmac, followed a moment later by the rear landing gear. James felt the whole vehicle tug downwards briefly before moving into a steady ascent.

'Mission Control, we have lift-off,' he said into his suit radio. 'Climbing. Handles like a dream, Captain.'

Five minutes passed and the *Aurora* breached the

stratosphere, the air-breathing turbojets driving the spacecraft hard. At fifteen kilometres the ground was a distant memory.

'Pushing past Mach one,' said James as the *Aurora* broke the sound barrier with a bang and continued unabated past Mach two and three. The roar of the engines was deafening and swelled all the more as the craft approached Mach four.

An unbearable whine developed inside the cockpit, and James winced. He quickly locked down the visor of his helmet to deaden the noise.

This wasn't in the simulations.

'Mission Control, I'm pushing to hypersonic. Why the hell is this ship so goddamned loud?'

Austin's laugh crackled through the radio. 'Horrible ain't it? There was a resonance we couldn't get rid of, but it won't do any harm. When you get above twenty-eight you can switch to rocket mode.'

The screens lit up, bathing the cockpit in green as Austin spoke, showing the *Aurora* passing beyond the twenty-eight kilometre mark and Mach five.

'Roger, Mission Control, closing the intakes now.'

'Go ahead, *Aurora*,' said Austin. 'Just watch out for the kick. Over.'

James grunted and flicked a switch on the dashboard, bracing himself against the back of his seat in the process. The screens showed the turbojet intakes close and switch over to the engine's propellant burning phase. It was the briefest moment of silence, no more than a millisecond. Then, with a thundering roar, the rocket engines ignited.

James's body became as lead and stuck fast to the chair, pressing hard as though willing itself to tunnel through it. Greater even than he had felt on the rocket to rendezvous with the *Magnum Opus*, the acceleration took him by surprise despite his readiness. All he could do was yelp as the numbers climbed. Even with his helmet on, the noise was deafening.

Within seconds, the *Aurora* reached its orbital velocity, passing through the mesosphere and into the thermosphere. The automated systems on the ship kicked in and turned the rocket engines off, halting the acceleration. Released from the Newtonian vice grip, James's arms floated free in microgravity. His chest ached as he inhaled so he reined in his arms and cradled his ribs.

The ship's automated systems, allowing James a moment's respite, pulsed the reaction control thrusters in preparation for orbital insertion. With a groan, James set the throttle back to its neutral position and toggled the flight stick to RCS mode. Watching the screens with keen eyes, he nudged the stick to and fro firing the appropriate ion thrusters, and brought the ship into a circular low Earth orbit.

All was quiet.

James sighed and removed his helmet, allowing it to float away in the cockpit briefly before securing it down. He closed his eyes and took in the tranquillity of the moment. When he opened them again and looked out of the front window, he saw nothing but stars. The cockpit was dark except for the lighted controls, yet the stars were dim in the glare of the Earth; the diffuse fringe of the atmosphere glowed in the triangular side windows. At the very edge of the window, the distant horizon bulged; deep blue with wisps of white.

I'd forgotten how beautiful this is.

He smiled and radioed for Mission Control using the controls on the dashboard. 'This is Commander James Fowler of the *IXS-17 Aurora* confirming successful insertion into LEO. Altitude four-ten, velocity seven-point-six-eight. The stars are bright and the Earth is beautiful. Over.'

'Roger that, *Aurora*,' said Austin. Groaning with excitement, he continued, 'You're making me jealous, man. I wish I could see it again. Now, the next stage is up to you. Take your time, get your bearings and then activate the flight computer's course for Neptune when you're ready. Over.'

'Copy that, Mission Control,' said James.

He unfastened his restraints and pushed himself off from the chair, floating towards the left window. He put his hands out either side of the frame to halt his movement, and pressed his face up against the glass. The condensation from his breath rose up the pane. As he stared in awe on the gleaming, azure planet below, he caught his breath as if seeing it for the first time: The Earth illuminated amid the blackness of the night sky like a candle in the dark; the cradle of humanity, seen on a such a scale that mankind could easily have not existed on it at all.

I remember!

James took a moment to appreciate and marvel. It was remarkably therapeutic as the years of bitterness retreated from his recaptured sense of wonder. He caught a glance of his dim reflection in the glass. His appearance hadn't changed in the last few hours; Angela had convinced him to keep the beard after all, but there was a new glint in his eye that changed his countenance. With a grin, he drifted back to the pilot's seat and secured himself down.

'Mission Control, I'm ready. Starting ion engine and pushing a bit higher,' James said, orienting the craft so it faced into its orbit before pushing forwards on the throttle control. He kept a close eye on the trajectory indicator, making course adjustments to maintain orbit and reduce speed.

'Altitude five-zero-zero, velocity seven-point-six-one-six. Mission Control, I am activating the flight computer and plotting the course for Neptune.'

He jabbed at some of the controls on the panel above him. The flight computer beeped, indicating a successful route plot. On the main screen was a diagram of the course. It was a straight shot to Neptune; the path was clear of other planets. The orbital positions of the four gas giants were arranged in a sort of cross, with Saturn in conjunction. Mars was also heading that way, so it would be a long while before there could be any new resupply missions to Arcadia Landing. That is, without ships like the *Aurora*.

If this mission succeeds, we need never worry about where the planets are in their orbits again.

'Course plot confirmed. Here goes nothing, I'm turning on the Austinium drive. This had better not blow up in my face, Captain.'

'Copy that, and hey, I am ninety-nine—uhh—eighty-three percent sure it's not gonna turn you into fried chicken. Over.'

Eighty-three! Oh god, please don't explode.

James reached out to the switch on the dashboard labelled 'plaid'. He gave a nervous chuckle and hovered his trembling finger underneath it for a moment. Squeezing his eyes shut, he flicked the switch and gritted his teeth. A low hum rose from the rear of the spacecraft, which was accompanied by the slightest rumble. He opened his eyes with a blink and released the tension in his jaw.

'Captain, I am eighty-three percent sure you're an arsehole. Over,' said James with a loud sigh. 'Spooling drive.'

He pressed the stiff metal button on the side of the throttle handle and the low hum rose to a comfortable whirr. On the dashboard a small orange light next to the 'plaid' switch blinked steadily. On it, printed in black, were the words, 'Ready to engage'.

James's heart raced and his breathing quickened. Beads of sweat clung to his brow in the microgravity, wobbling to and fro. He gripped the throttle and stick, now engaged into their third mode: for manipulating the Austinium drive's warp field.

His voice shook as he said, 'Drive spooled, controls switched over. Ready to go.'

'Roger, *Aurora*. Got any poignant last words? Over.'

'Not this time, mate. I'm absolutely bricking it. Maybe just… Stick the kettle on, I'll be back in time for tea.'

Without a second thought, James pushed the throttle open to maximum with a thud. For a moment, all remained still. With a furrowed brow, James craned his neck as much as he could, squinting into the night. It seemed the drive didn't work after all.

Poor Austin. Nearly twenty years of work. Back to the drawing board, I guess.

Wait a minute…

There was something out there, but he wasn't sure what it was. There appeared a faint wobble in the stars, a twinkle, as if looking up at them through the Earth's atmosphere. The twinkle became like a ripple in a puddle from a raindrop, and then from a hailstone. As he began to comprehend the impossible disturbance across the immutable sky, his eyes widened. The ripples morphed at speed into a vertical stretch; the universe was elastic, pulled from both ends by unseen hands. James clamped his eyes shut and made to shield himself. There was a faint sizzling as the stretching effect reached its limit.

Crack!

CHAPTER FIVE
Disappearance

It was chaos back at Mission Control. The real-time telemetry from the *Aurora* had cut out after Commander Fowler engaged the ship's faster-than-light engine. Cameras tracking the ship aboard Skyport showed a bright flash of light in that same moment.

Austin had expected to be able to continue tracking the *Aurora* until it exceeded light speed. The immediate cut to communications was a cause for concern. The energy of the flash suggested an explosion, and that the spaceplane had been vaporised in the blast.

He refused to believe it and set his staff to the task of finding a way to re-establish contact.

Flight controllers and support personnel ran up and down the aisles, all trying this or that solution. They checked outside on their radio equipment, and rebooted computer systems. Paperwork flew everywhere and plenty of cups of coffee were spilled in the fray.

The director stood at the back of the room, staring dumbfounded at the readouts on the large screen, watching the mayhem unfold as if in slow motion. Sweat poured from his perfectly preened face, now pallid at the prospect of having sent the Commander to his death. The screen took up the entire front wall of the Mission Control Centre, and displayed the last known co-ordinates of the *Aurora* before its signal was lost.

Austin sat at a workstation with a headset half on his ears, shouting down the attached microphone. Between driving himself hoarse and frantically tuning to different radio frequencies, he restarted his terminal, desperate to kick the software into establishing a connection.

'*Aurora*, this is Mission Control, do you read me?' he repeated. 'Do you read me, *Aurora*? This is Mission Control. Come in.' He slammed his fist down on the desk. 'James! I swear if you're playing me, we're through, you hear? Goddammit, Jimmy, answer me. Where the fuck are you?'

Midway through repeating his message for the umpteenth time, he felt a tap on his shoulder. Glancing sidelong at the flight controller next to him, he shook the hand away and continued his calls.

The flight controller's hand appeared on his arm again. At his touch, Austin, his face now bright red with rage, grabbed the headphones from his head and smashed them on the desktop sending bits of plastic flying.

'Riley, what?' he roared, rounding on the hapless flight controller. 'What the fuck is so important that you've stopped—'

The terrified-looking Riley gestured to one of the doors at the back of the room with a trembling hand.

Austin followed the finger. The see-through door was ajar and Angela stood in the gap gripping the frame, watching with a look of horror and confusion.

Austin's face fell and his stomach churned; shame replaced anger, and he went cold with dread.

'Shit.'

Angela caught his gaze and started towards him, manoeuvring through the rows of disconnected desks and around the rushing staff.

Looking to the floor, he rose to meet her.

'What the hell is going on, Austin?' Her voice trembled as she stood before him and glanced around the room.

Austin fiddled with his hands and tears welled up in his eyes. His voice, already hoarse from yelling, broke as he looked up at her. 'I—I'm so sorry, Angie. There was a flash and we, uhh'—he sniffed—'we lost contact with Jimmy.'

'What do you mean "lost contact"? Flash? Wha—' The panic in Angela's voice was palpable. She looked this way and that. The flight controllers spoke loud and urgently as they worked at their stations, creating a din.

'In truth, we don't know what happened,' said Austin. His words brought Angela's wayward gaze back on him with frightening intensity. Nevertheless, he continued, 'This wasn't in any of our models or tests... We're trying to re-establish contact now. But the preliminary analysis is not looking good.'

'Not looking good? You don't think he's...'

'I don't wanna believe it, Angie. All's I'm saying is I think we need to be prepared for the worst.'

Angela mouthed his words back at him, still staring, the intense blue of her eyes like lightning.

Faster than a blink, her hand came up and slapped Austin hard across the cheek.

He reeled back with a yelp and stumbled into the desk. The room went silent. All eyes in the Mission Control Centre were now on them.

'How could you?' Angela screeched, her words interspersed with heaving sobs. 'We trusted—I fucking trusted you, Austin!' She whirled away for a moment then stepped back and came up close to Austin's face as he tried to stand. 'When James started getting cold feet, I told him, oh Jesus, I told him you wouldn't steer him wrong. He believed in your vision and now you're telling me he could be dead?'

Austin rubbed his cheek and tears filled his eyes. He opened his mouth but Angela cut him off. The shouting had subsided, replaced by quiet bitterness, edged with rage.

'You were our friend. No-one else on this godforsaken planet but you knows what we went through all those years ago. How could you? You were his friend and you've killed him.'

Angela turned on her heel and marched off back through the plexiglass doorway, shoving a flight controller aside as she went.

Still holding the side of his face, Austin continued to stare long after she was gone.

That was never gonna go well...

He didn't blame her. Angela's every word had cut like a knife. She was right; he felt the weight of his responsibility for James's disappearance keenly. There was no other way around it: beguiled by Austin's tantalising vision of the future, James had paid the ultimate price.

Austin knew his immortal friend hated the idea of living forever, but that didn't mean he wanted to die.

I guess the Achelon get the last laugh after all.

Suddenly Austin became aware of the stillness in the Mission Control Centre. No-one had moved or spoken throughout Angela's tirade, or since.

Resolving to go after her, he made to leave, taking up his jacket from the back of his chair. He'd barely taken one step when a hand clasped his upper arm and he turned. Flight controller Ilona Illes looked down at him with concern, her green eyes had the same piercing intensity as Angela's. She was taller than Austin, even seated.

'Captain, you're needed here in case we get a signal,' she said. 'I'll go talk to her instead.'

'But you don't even know her.'

'True, but we have met, at least. Look, I know what she's going through, and you're way too close to it yourself, sir.'

Austin stared at her for a long moment, then relented. Silently, he slumped into his chair. 'You're right. I'm better off here. Y'know, I've never actually spoken to Angie alone? Always Jimmy there. Every time we met was always about mine or James's work. I don't know her as well as I ought, and I ain't the best person to comfort her now.'

Ilona knelt beside Austin and placed a hand on his shoulder. 'Leave her with me. That anger she's feeling? Not about you. You concentrate on finding her husband.'

'Thanks Ilona.'

* * *

Angela sat alone in silence at the end of the stark grey corridor. Diffuse light filtered through the frosted window. She stared up at the blur of shapes and colours in the glass, her jaw set and fists balled in her lap, as tears traced lines down her cheeks.

It's all my fault.

The deep ache penetrated her soul and she winced as pangs of guilt came on thick and fast. She thought back to when they first heard from Lieutenant Colonel Dryden, how she had persuaded James to get back on his feet and take the job. He'd been stuck in a rut for so long, she had convinced herself he needed the push. And so she pushed. At every expression of doubt, she had brought him around and filled him with hope and purpose, rekindling his passion like blowing on a spark. It seemed a good idea at the time. Instead, she had been enticing him towards the flame like a temptress whispering that the fire is good, and now he had been consumed by the inferno.

So wrapped up in her thoughts, she barely perceived the cautious click-clack of shoes approaching her, until they stopped.

She tore her sightless gaze away from the colours in the window. It was Ilona, the flight controller Angela and James had met their first day on base. She'd seen her around in the Mission Control Centre, but hadn't spoken to her since that first day.

'Hi, Mrs Fowler, I don't know if you remember me, my name's Ilona,' said the woman, taking a tentative step forward as she gave a little wave. 'I saw what happened back there. You looked like you could use someone to talk to.'

'I'm fine,' said Angela, looking away with a sniff, '... thank you.'

Ilona stood in silence for a long moment before she sat in the chair next to Angela. 'I get it, all this, y'know? The anger, the pain... the guilt. I'm here if you want to talk.'

Who was this captivating younger woman? Angela sighed and flexed her fingers in their tight fists. She wasn't used to bottling away her emotions, but neither did she want to dump everything on this person she'd barely spoken to.

Her attempt at concealment became futile as a hand appeared on hers, sending a pleasant tingle up her arm along with a sense of safety, and she blurted, 'I did this. He wouldn't have gone up in that damn thing if wasn't for me. And now he's gone.'

'Feels that way, huh?'

'I killed him, as surely as if I had detonated the ship myself.'

'That's one way to look at it, I suppose,' said Ilona, scooting closer but removing her hand. 'But I can tell you from personal experience, you're wrong.'

Angela wheeled around at her, expecting a mocking grin, but instead met with the kindly smile of a pained soul and fellow traveller on the pathways of grief.

'Have you...?' Angela started.

Ilona nodded. 'My girlfriend died three years ago. Killed by a couple of young thugs breaking into our home.' She sighed and looked down into her lap. 'So many things went wrong that day. We argued, I was late for work here, I forgot to lock the door behind me. She came home in the middle of the break-in and one of them got scared and stabbed her.'

'My god, that's horrible!'

'Yeah. For the longest time I blamed myself for not locking that door. That it was my carelessness, caused by my own pettiness in starting that stupid argument, that had killed her. But I came to realise that's not how the world works. That guy made a choice; I didn't choose for him. I didn't put the knife in his hand, and I didn't persuade him to use force when he could've run away like his friend. That was all on him. And this is not on you.'

'Austin—'

'No! This is not on anyone who's tried their best to do right by the Commander, nor on the Commander himself. He went into this knowing full well what the risks were. I know what these people around here are like—the ones who have gone to space—they do it with open eyes, gladly accepting the risk that something may go wrong because their passion is to build us a better future out there. Now, tell me the Commander is any different.'

Angela thought back to James's words during the hologram recording.

'I don't blame anyone. Not you, Angela, Austin, or the ISA... Whatever happens, know that I counted the risk and it was worth it.'

She's right. I'm giving myself far too much credit for making James do this.

'Besides,' said Ilona. 'We don't really know what happened yet. The tech teams are working on theories, but until we know for sure, we're going to keep looking for him.'

'Thank you.' After wiping away her tears with her

fingers, Angela examined Ilona more closely. 'Who are you anyway? I mean I know you're from Mission Control and all, but I don't know anything about you. I appreciate you coming to see me, but... why?'

Ilona smiled. Her cheeks flushed and she rubbed the back of her neck. 'I'm actually a fan of your work,' she stammered. 'I've watched your livestreams a few times, and I love your poetry books.'

Angela perked up. 'Small world. I didn't think I'd meet anyone who knows who I am here.'

'Weird, right? I didn't expect to run into you here either. I've been meaning to introduce myself for a while. Then when this happened, I thought you might appreciate a friendly face.'

'I think I need to take my mind off of things,' Angela said, shifting sideways and lifting her foot onto the chair. It was a hard seat, but she did her best to get comfy. 'And you *do* have a friendly face. So, tell me about yourself, Ilona.'

With a wide grin, Ilona said, 'Okay, well I'm thirty-eight years old; I live over in Tatabánya nowadays, which is north of here. You might already have guessed, but I'm bi—'

'I sort of figured; so am I. You actually remind me of an old girlfriend from my university days.'

Ilona gave her an appreciative look and continued, 'A friend introduced me to your streams because he knows I'm a big reader and poetry resonates with me more than fiction, you know?'

'That's an interesting contrast. I sort of assumed everyone around here would be into sci-fi.'

'Oh, I'm into the *science*, but not so much the fiction.'

The two talked animatedly for another twenty minutes. Angela's mood had settled from being given a welcome, if brief, reprieve from her worries. The isolation of grief was the worst thing, and she was thankful for Ilona's presence.

After a while Angela suggested she should probably apologise to Austin. Ilona agreed to accompany her back to the Mission Control Centre, both to give her some support and to check on their progress locating James.

* * *

Journalists and newscasters crowded the Mission Control Centre. They stood in the corners of the room, filled the foyer and corridors, and generally got under everyone's feet. All were reporting the same story into their broadcast cameras.

'Pandemonium, right here in Budapest,' the special correspondent said, pointing behind him at the scramble. 'Earlier today, the International Space Administration carried out the inaugural flight of the *Aurora*, the experimental spaceplane that was revealed to the world three months ago, carrying a revolutionary new propulsion system. In his impromptu press conference back in August, the ISA director, Dr Konstantinu Azzopardi, promised the *Aurora* would herald a new era of space exploration for humankind. However, recent events tell a very different story.

'At seven in the evening local time, the Mission Control Centre lost contact with the *Aurora* and its lone pilot, Commander James Fowler, after engaging the new drive system. Staff and crews here at the MCC are still clinging to hope, desperately trying to find out what happened, what went wrong, and whether the unanticipated signal loss means the test was successful or a catastrophic failure.

'If they cannot regain contact in the next few hours, we may have to accept the loss of yet another fine, young astronaut. This is Chuks Kisakye for BBC World News. Back to the studio.'

Standing off to one side with the director, Austin tore his weary gaze from Kisakye. With a grave look about him, he glanced sidelong at Dr Azzopardi. 'I still can't get anything over radio, I've tried every frequency,' he said, keeping his voice low.

Dr Azzopardi frowned. 'We cannot give in, Captain. Are we any closer to a workable theory about what happened? Could it have been sabotage? One of Guy Furious's supporters?'

Austin shook his head. 'Believe me, sir, I ain't giving in. There's just nothing more I can do from here. Look, I know the flash looked like an explosion, but it could easily have been something else.'

'Like what?' asked the Director.

'We won't know for sure until the folks at LIGO get back to us with their data. If they've spotted a gravitational wave around the time of that flash, then I'd bet my last dollar Jimmy's alright.'

'Okay, how long?'

Before he could answer, Angela and Ilona arrived in the MCC and made a beeline for them. Austin remained silent, and watched Angela with caution.

'Any progress?' said Angela.

Austin noted with relief that her tone was surprisingly

steady; she spoke as though nothing had happened. Gone was the former ferocity that had brought her wrath down on him. Whatever Ilona said to her had helped.

'No,' said Austin, finally. 'I was just telling the director we're waiting for data from LIGO.'

'Are you sure it could not have been sabotage?' said the director. 'We have seen this before with the uncrewed launch, and there was that young reporter from the press conference talking about the cults.'

Austin pinched the bridge of his nose. 'No, security's tight. No-one's had access to the *Aurora* who hasn't already been vetted, and the spectral analysis of the flash shows it can't have been a bomb.'

'Could they have tampered with the drive itself?' Angela asked.

'Not a chance.' said Austin, shaking his head. 'I wouldn't credit a single one of the idiots in any of those groups with the know-how to turn it into an explosive. I know, because I've made one blow up myself. It's one of the first damn things we fixed.'

'I've been thinking,' said Ilona, looking between the director and Austin. 'Hear me out. What if the *Aurora*'s warp field cut the signal?'

'Impossible,' said Austin. 'We tested for that sort of thing. We could always get a signal through in the lab.'

'But, sir,' she pressed. 'How strong was the field in the lab? We know the drive produces an extreme string-thin distortion in spacetime—' She turned to Angela. 'It's what stops it becoming a gravity well of its own—' Looking back at Austin, she continued, 'but at the kind of strength necessary to move a whole spacecraft, it might also be what's preventing a signal getting through in either direction.'

'Like an event horizon?'

'Exactly. The expanded region of spacetime in the field behind the ship will redshift away our signals, and anything in front will be blue-shifted and accumulate. Plus, as soon as the *Aurora* goes above light speed, it'll outpace our messages anyway.'

Austin put his hands on his hips and stared at her for a long moment. 'If you're right then we'll be waiting hours before we can re-establish contact.'

'Yes, we'd have to wait until he arrives in orbit around Neptune and tries to radio us. If the Austinium drive manages to make top speed, we're talking about six hours at the very least.'

'I am not convinced,' the director said, starting to walk away. 'We keep trying to either get through or locate the debris, and we will see what happens in six hours.'

Angela, Austin and Ilona stood in relative silence for a long moment; the discomfort was tangible, and after a while Ilona nudged Angela with her elbow.

She hesitated and then took a tentative step closer to Austin.

'I'm sorr—'

The old captain held up his hand immediately. 'I accept. I get what you're going through, Angie. I don't blame you for gettin' mad. You were right, this is my fault.'

'No. No it's not,' Angela shook her head and sighed. 'No-one anticipated this happening, and I know you would never have let James get in that spacecraft if there was even the slightest hint this could go wrong. I said some truly awful things, and I'm sorry.'

The two stared at one another, their eyes red and

damp. Then they embraced, hugging one another tightly, and Angela sobbed into Austin's shoulder.

'We'll get him back, Angie. We'll get him back.'

CHAPTER SIX
BEYOND THE LIMIT

JAMES BLINKED AND LOWERED HIS ARMS. The view out of the front of the ship had returned to normal, or, as normal as could be expected given the circumstances. The stars had, at the very least, snapped back into place. But out of the side windows the sky was distorted as if looking through the bottom of a glass bottle; the light of thousands of stars twisted and turned as the *Aurora*'s warp field oscillated.

He peered at the screen. His velocity was climbing rapidly. Metres-per-second turned to kilometres; kilometres became megametres, but out of the window there was nothing, save for the ring of lensing stars that encircled the ship. If the readout on the screen was to be believed, the *Aurora* was accelerating, but he felt nothing. He couldn't tell he was moving at all. It was another strange sensation in a day filled with strange sensations. His eyes darted from the screen to the view and back.

This is nothing like the simulations. Then again, I guess I'm the first to see how this really looks.

In the opposite corner of the screen was a small zero where his speed had been measured prior to activating the Austinium drive.

I'm not really moving. Yet, I am. I'm now sitting in the fastest man-made object in history and I'm still sub-light.

At thirty megametres-per-second, the readout on the screen changed again, giving way to a decimal with an italicised '*c*'.

Ten percent of the speed of light.

He reached over to the communications panel and pressed the broadcast button, speaking into his suit's microphone.

'Mission Control, this is the *Aurora*. It was touch-and-go for a moment there but all systems appear to be working nominally. The drive is active and the instruments are telling me I'm going point-two-five-*c*. It's so weird: I can't feel a thing!' James said.

He waited a few seconds. There was no response from Mission Control, just the slight crackle of static over the open channel.

I've come pretty far; I'm already past the moon, but their signal should still reach me. Unless…

The stellar backdrop to the front of the spaceplane had begun to fade, the crisp points of light slowly dimming in a faint bluish haze.

Unless the warp field is somehow interfering with comms. Damn. If that's true, I'll be alone the whole time I'm in this bubble.

The more he considered Austin's teaching on the drive's operation, the more his theory made sense. At one third light speed, the blueshift to the front was unmistakable as the steady light of stars—and even that of the cosmic microwave background—unperturbed for billions of years, had their wavelengths compressed into a higher-energy state by the field's bow wave. There, they accumulated like swarms of bugs covering a windshield. It stood to reason any signals from Earth would suffer a similar but opposing fate when striking the wall of sheared spacetime from the rear, their energies diminished to almost nothing.

Pretty soon I won't be able to see out the front at all.

The numbers on the screen continued climbing. James reached out and flicked through the different displays until he reached one showing the ship's course in relation to the rest of the solar system. The *Aurora* was a little point, yet barely a hair's-breadth along its path to the Ice Giant.

Tentatively, James unbuckled himself and floated closer to the side window to get a better look at the ring of gravitational distortion around the ship. He turned away after a few seconds and shook his head; the sight gave him a headache. He pulled himself back down towards the seat to get a look at the telemetry again.

Fifty percent.

Sixty percent.

Seventy-five percent.

The oscillations around the ship swam more violently, and the dancing stars changed pace from their slow waltz into a chaotic quickstep.

The numbers ticked over, much more slowly than before and this gave James a sudden pit in his stomach. What if the Austinium drive failed to push the *Aurora* beyond the limit? He was already going faster than any human in history, faster than any deep-space probe. Staying sub-light would still have a revolutionary effect on human exploration of the solar system, but presented a problem for interstellar ventures. Where could humankind go if the cosmic speed limit was an impassable line even for the Austinium drive? The next closest star would always be more than four years away.

James sighed as he watched the deepening blue fog that now encompassed the entire forward view. People would still go, of course; four or five years is better than twenty thousand. Single expeditions could even stretch to expend half a human lifetime. But venturing further would require generation ships and, for the most extreme interstellar distances, the Austinium drive's greatest strength—its complete ignorance of relativistic time dilation—would become undesirable.

Ninety percent.

Faster-than-light is our gateway to the future without having to make compromises.

In the late twentieth century, when people first started to speculate about the possibility of a warp drive, one of the main arguments against creating such a device was the idea that humanity would need to already have access to one in order to make it. No-one could have imagined that just such an occurrence would actually happen.

Ninety-five percent.

James gripped the back of his chair as he floated, staring at the screen, sweating. His heart raced, but this time for the suspense and excitement. He'd already broken records with this flight, but all of that paled into insignificance at the prospect of breaching the hard barrier for all things that carried mass.

As the ship approached light speed, the light of the stars now stretched out in a swirling tumult of jagged lines, and then without any fanfare—or thankfully, cataclysm—the decimals ticked over to One.

Is that it? Wait... Wow!

Where before the ring of stars had been a stream of churning chaos, now they danced lightly, almost rhythmically. Instead of being headache-inducing, James found himself mesmerised watching the ballet of the universe unfold around the little spaceplane. Mouth agape and breath fogging up the glass, he didn't want to look away. Forcing himself out of his captivation, he floated back down and strapped in.

A quick glance to the screen made him catch his breath. His velocity now read as one-point-one, and then it moved up to one-point-two. For a long moment he stared all agog, then he drummed his fingers triumphantly on the dashboard.

In his excitement he moved to open a broadcast channel but thought better of it. Perhaps he could record something to send after he arrived at Neptune? He set about looking through the on-screen menus. After a short while hunting he found the option to store an audio recording for later transmission.

'Mission Control, this is the *Aurora*. The drive works. I repeat: the drive bloody works! By the time you receive this I'll have been at Neptune for a few hours, but as of this recording the ship's hit light speed and damn well sailed right past it.' He cleared his throat and calmed his breathing before continuing, 'I'm registering a velocity of one-point-five-*c* and it just keeps going up. Point seven... eight... nine... Oh, it's stopped. Velocity is now holding steady at two-*c*.' James leaned away from the screen and laughed loud. 'Twice the speed of light! Austin, you crazy old git, you did it.'

He paused the recording and pulled a small blue notebook and pen from a compartment next to the dashboard. After a few minutes scribbling and mumbling to himself, he smiled and tapped the screen with the end of the pen.

'Thought so,' he said, starting the recording again. 'Looks like it'll take me about two hours from now to get to Neptune. I'll be sending this recording when I get there. I'm sure you've all figured it out by now but the warp field is scrambling all incoming and outgoing signals, so it'll be six hours before you get this message.

'Suffice to say, this is a momentous achievement. Congratulations, Captain.'

James woke to the sound of a soft alarm in the cockpit and arched his back in a stretch that made him groan. Relying on the automatic pilot and guidance systems, he had busied himself by taking a well-earned nap.

The *Aurora* had cruised at top-speed through empty space for the past two hours with the same harmonious stellar dance going on outside. After recording his message for Mission Control, there was truly nothing for James to do, nothing for him to see, no oddities to report on. Just the rest of the journey to stare at blue haze and shimmering stars.

He rubbed the sleep from his eyes and yawned. The course readout showed he was nearing the end of his journey. He'd set the alarm to wake him in enough time to make the necessary speed and attitude adjustments. The last thing he wanted was to fly past his destination. He'd done that a few times during his simulation training. It turned out the *Aurora* at FTL had a turning circle the size of a planet and handled like a manatee. Mercifully, Austin's team had the good sense to tie the orientation of the warp field to that of the ship's vector, so it would always be pointing in its direction of travel. But still, having to loop around, or even drop from FTL and come about, would have added a lot more travel time.

After making a quick check of his seat restraints, he eased back on the throttle control. As his speed dropped below the light barrier, the blue haze began to fade and the stars once again came into view. Neptune was now within visual range. At first it appeared tiny, no bigger than Mars or the Earth; a miniscule point in the darkness surrounded by its myriad moons. The tiny orb grew in size until, after a matter of seconds, it filled view.

Wow!

The Ice Giant hung magnificent in its deep blue which, from up close, was far from uniform. Dark bands of cloud ringed the latitudes close to the poles, and small wisps of white methane-ice cirrus dotted the planet's tropopause, churned up by deeper windstorms.

With the Austinium drive still engaged, he slowed the *Aurora* to a relative crawl: a mere thirty kilometres-per-second, and he stared transfixed at the strange, alien world as the hairs on his arms and the back of his neck tingled.

His gaze was drawn to the most distinguishing feature on the surface: the gargantuan navy storm at the equator.

Easily as large as the Earth itself, the Great Dark Spot was one of the many relatively short-lived giant storms the planet had hosted over the aeons.

Incredible... The Voyager images don't do it justice.

Encircling the planet, far beyond the bounds of its atmosphere, and stretched out before the *Aurora*, faint rings reflected dimly the light of the distant sun. The small icy moons, Naiad, Thalassa and Despina were barely visible in the gap between its Galle and Le Verrier rings.

Blowing out a long breath as he melted into the seat, James recalled the warm September nights he had spent in the garden as a child, looking through his father's telescope at Neptune and its largest moon, Triton. Mark Fowler's deep love for space and science had captured James's imagination from an early age and instilled the passion that drove him to become an astronaut.

He cherished the bond they shared even into adulthood. The look of pride in his father's face when James told him he had been chosen for the ESA's astronaut programme still warmed his heart. Both of his parents had died a few years ago: his mother, Esther, from cancer, and his father from pneumonia.

Somehow, seeing Neptune up-close felt like he had brought his relationship with his father full-circle; it gave him more closure than he'd had from the funeral.

You'd have loved to have seen this, dad.

Opening up the throttle once again, but keeping his speed low, James manoeuvred the Aurora further into the Neptunian system, gliding in above the Lassel Ring and skirting along it. At this close distance, the plane of the half-kilometre thick layer of debris seemed to go on forever and chunks of varying sizes whooshed by as they passed under the ship. He'd descended as far as he dared. There was no telling what would happen should he enter the rings themselves at this speed, and he didn't want to get riddled with micrometeorites.

Making a close pass of Despina, he took in its misshapen, pockmarked surface, noting every striation, crater and ridge down to the minutest detail. Then finally tearing his gaze from the tiny moon, he pulled the ship back up above the equatorial plane and headed further out towards Triton.

The Aurora might handle like a ten-ton-turd, but this sure is fun.

He let out an involuntary laugh. Manipulation of the *Aurora*'s warp field gave James a level of control over his speed that astounded him.

In only a few minutes, he was further out and approaching the system's largest moon. Far from the small white spot that he'd seen with averted vision through his father's telescope, Triton's surface was richly detailed with outcrops and plateaus and plains of ice, though little to be seen in the way of cratering.

He brought the craft into a low equatorial orbit and the ship passed over regions of cryovolcanism, spewing water-ice high into the moon's thin atmosphere.

It was here James disengaged the Austinium drive with another loud crack and stabilised his orbit. Neptune itself sat in splendour out of one window, while Triton's surface passed by out of another. Triton was much closer to its azure parent than the Earth to the Moon, and at four-times the size of Earth, Neptune loomed large in the sky above its captive satellite.

James pressed switches on the dashboard. There was

a motorised whirr as a small bay at the front of the craft opened. The bay contained a suite of sensors and cameras which he set to the task of recording images and taking readings of the moon's surface. He then broadcast his previously-recorded message to Earth.

There was a light ping confirming the data burst had completed and he moved to open the channel again for a live broadcast, but hesitated. What would he say? He'd seen so much he wanted to share in so short a time that he was fit to burst.

No, no… best keep this as professional as I can.

He took a moment slow his breathing and gather his thoughts before pressing the button.

'Mission Control, th—this is the *Aurora*. I have arrived at Neptune in orbit of Triton and I'm preparing preliminary scans. You'll have received my previous message a few minutes ago, but Captain, I don't know how to congratulate you enough: the drive works perfectly, no issues to report. I'm alive, well and the ship is intact. Over.'

He considered for a moment the significance of his journey. Conventionally the trip would have taken years and would have required a carefully planned route of gravitational slingshots around the other planets.

This Achelon technology… I wonder how long it would've taken us to develop it ourselves?

James scoffed and shook his head as if arguing with himself. It was an insult to Austin and his team to call this drive system alien. He may have followed the formulas in their database, but there was no doubt about it: this was Earth tech.

Despite all that, I get why people are afraid we're bringing wrath down upon ourselves.

It was a strange feeling, understanding Guy Furious's point of view. Humanity had descended like vultures, pillaging anything and everything from the corpses of beings so much more advanced they might has well have been gods. Some, like the cultists, did regard them as such. Either way, fear was fear. Guy Furious had coined a phrase altogether by accident out of auto-translated Latin which had become a sort-of motto among some of his more hardline supporters, 'Sit sidera silere: Let the stars remain silent.'

He shook his head again. No, there would be no wrath. The communications equipment on the alien warship had been broken beyond repair. There was no way the ship could have sent a message even if it wanted to, and that meant no retribution, no smiting, no attack fleets coming from beyond the darkness.

Stealing another glance at the giant world, he watched as the terminator line crept across its surface causing Triton and the *Aurora* to slip into night. James removed his gloves and laced his hands behind his head as the yellow glow of far-off sunlight descended, scattering its rays through the backlit atmosphere; a magnificent alien sunset.

Besides, all this... Might just be worth it.

CHAPTER SEVEN
Relief

Austin drummed his fingers on the desk and groaned as he stared at the enormous screen on the wall. His eyes stung and he leaned heavily, cupping his head in the other hand. The flight controllers had put up a countdown timer with their best estimate of when the Commander would arrive at Neptune, and Austin refused to take his eyes off it.

The activity in the Mission Control Centre had calmed over the course of the last six hours. Most of the journalists had moved on, with the exception of one eager young reporter from a local news station who had opted to stay in the hopes of being the first to claim any update.

A weedy figure of a man—overdressed for the occasion—he'd spent the first few hours cosying up to the director. Austin had watched with amusement as Dr Azzopardi rebuffed him with only a contemptuous scowl.

It was far less amusing, however, when the kid came

over to Austin instead; he was far too busy to deal with that nonsense. So he took a leaf out of the director's book and glowered at the young journalist, ignoring his incessant questioning until he went away.

A knot began to form in Austin's stomach when he saw the kid approach Angela. He thought about calling him back and agreeing to answer the damn questions as long as he stayed away from her, but the knot quickly loosened as she rounded on the kid and curtly told him where he could stick his camera drone. As the young journalist retreated to go and bother somebody else, Austin turned away and chuckled to himself.

Mercifully, the journalist had given up after the fourth hour and now sat asleep in the corner of the room, his phone dangling from his limp fingers.

It was late, or rather, early in the morning of the sixteenth of November and the lights had been dimmed for the night shift. The centre was now operating on a rotating skeleton crew, allowing the flight controllers time to rest. Only Austin, Angela, Ilona and Dr Azzopardi had remained throughout. The timer showed half an hour to go until the earliest they could expect to receive a transmission from the spacecraft and its wayward pilot. After Ilona's suggestion about the Austinium drive cutting off communications, the team had continued actively searching for another two hours. A search which turned up nothing.

LIGO had returned its results around the fifth hour, showing a gravitational wave detection at the same moment as the supposed explosion. It didn't rule out destruction, but it fell in line with Ilona's theory, and with Austin's hope. It wasn't much, but it was a glimmer, and that was enough.

Austin jolted awake. He'd been up for so long and the time had been tedious; surely a micro-sleep could be forgiven?

Angela giggled from behind him. 'Have a nice nap?'

'I wasn't sleeping,' Austin said, his speech slurred, 'I was just resting my eyes.'

'Yeah, until your elbow slipped off the desk.'

With a grumble Austin blinked the sleep away and looked to the main screen. Five minutes remained.

By now everyone in the Centre was staring at him. The only one who hadn't stirred was the sleeping journalist.

'It's getting near time, Captain,' said the director as he shuffled towards them. 'I am very sorry, but it seems it is time to accept the Commander is lost to us.'

'No!' said Angela. Her voice shook. 'He's still got a few minutes.'

'The timer was set for the shortest possible deadline, sir,' said Austin through clenched teeth, glancing sidelong at the director. 'If there is a transmission, it will depend when Jimmy sent it.'

But if Azzopardi's right... Damn it, if I hadn't insisted, you'd still be here, Jimmy.

'We will give it the full time,' said the director, 'and then I suggest we take a few days to process. Mrs Fowler, my sincerest apologies. Captain, I will see you on Wednesday and we will discuss the future of the project.'

'What future?' Austin shot up and winced as a familiar pain zipped through his back. 'This was it. I'm not risking someone else on another test fli—'

The director held up his hand. 'Wednesday.'

Austin took a step forward but Angela placed a hand on his shoulder and shook her head.

The timer on the screen reached zero. The three remained silent as the numbers blinked.

Austin let out a long, low sigh and nodded his head. He leaned over his desk and shut down the computer, clattering the mouse.

'No...' said Angela, backing away. 'No, no, no this can't be it. Austin? It can't be.'

Austin's heart was heavy. He heard her pleas, but he couldn't bear to look at her as rivulets ran down his cheeks, soaking into his beard.

What a fool I was.

'Wait everyone!'

Austin sniffed at the noise that came from the other end of the room. Wiping his eyes, he allowed himself to glance over to its source.

Brad Tyler, one of the remaining flight controllers, jumped up from his desk, his arms flailing. 'I've got something!'

Angela and Austin rushed over to his terminal.

'Whaddya got Tyler? Spill it, son,' said Austin, leaning heavily on the back of the chair, which creaked under his weight.

'Uhh, it's faint, sir. Real faint. But I started receiving static a moment ago.'

'Static?' said Angela as she leaned in and slammed her palm on the desk. 'That all you got?'

Tyler stammered, and his eyes darted between the two of them. 'No, I'm getting a transmission too. It's just starting to come through proper.'

Austin shook the back of the chair and roared, 'Then put it on the damn speakers!'

'Y—yes, sir!'

Austin's eyes widened and he breathed as if for the first time as he listened to the broken, choppy words coming over the system, interspersed with static. Angela dropped to her knees and sobbed.

'Mission control, this is—*kzzt*—drive works... At Neptune... few hours. Ship's hit light—*kzzt*—sailed right past it. Velocity... two-*c*. You crazy old git—*kzzt*.'

* * *

After the scans of Triton had completed, James moved the *Aurora* back to a high Neptunian orbit with its ion engines, passing above the giant's northern hemisphere within the inner ring. He'd spent the last few hours trying to recalibrate a particularly uncooperative magnetometer that had been thrown out when he reactivated the ship's multispectral scanner.

Sunrise above Neptune: just as spectacular as its sunset.
He'd torn himself away from the utterly riveting flood of raw sensor data scrolling over the screen to admire the ethereal alien dawn. The on-board high resolution camera took footage as the small bright dot of the sun set the edge of the atmosphere ablaze with its golden light.

The night had felt long and daybreak was welcome; the night-side of the planet was almost entirely pitch dark. With its form filling the majority of the view out of the window, Neptune's shadow, falling like a cloak over the *Aurora*, also blocked out most other sights of potential interest in the night sky. All James could do was watch the data pour in and wrestle with the magnetic field sensor. It was terribly dull; the data would have been fascinating if it hadn't been in its raw form.

The ship's sensors were monitoring a variety of interesting things: gravitational pull; atmospheric composition; ambient radiation; and, after some coaxing, the magnetic field strength, but James wasn't able to see or do much of anything with the data. His job was to collect it and bring it back to Earth for processing.

Yula was great with all this stuff. If she were still alive she'd have come along too and demanded a processing suite. Hell, she'd have done it all manually if she had to.

James chuckled to himself as he watched the rim of the atmosphere burn in the morning light. No sooner had the tiny star risen—almost lost amongst the cosmic background—than James's radio crackled. A voice came through, broken at first, then cleared.

'*Aurora*, this is Mission Control. Boy are we glad to hear your voice, Jimmy,' said Austin, his voice light and full of energy. 'Things have been going all sorts of crazy here. Thought we'd lost you in the flash. At least now we know to expect a comms blackout for your return trip.

'Excellent work making it all the way out there, by the way. I won't remind you what you need to do next; I'm sure you're already underway. Just send us another message before you head back, and make sure to wait the four hours or you'll overtake the transmission!'

Oops.

James's finger hovered over the transmitter. Taking the communications delay into account hurt his head. On the *Magnum* he'd left that kind of thing to the Captain, or to Major Zhu—not that he'd had any cause to send a transmission himself anyway—and even then they were only dealing with delays of a few minutes. Here it was much longer and the idea he could outrun the signal by a factor of two was mind-bending. With that kind of timing, he could send his reply, finish the job and get back home before they even knew he was coming. He retreated his hand from the button.

'Right,' he said to himself, making an effort to slap his thighs. His bare hands made a dull, unsatisfying flump on the suit padding, but he accepted it. 'No point replying now. Might as well finish up first. Then I'll only have to wait two hours before making a move.'

The ship was well into the planet's day side now, so James set to work imaging. Over the course of the next couple of hours he took wide shots in a variety of wavelengths and zoomed in on fine cloud details. The swirling storms which created patterns in the methane-tinted atmosphere were fascinating to watch. There was subtlety here amid the varying hues of blue that wasn't visible from further out. Fractal patterns that went down to the minutest detail: cells and storms, whiffs and wisps; variations and layers that made Neptune just as much a jewel as its flashier cousins. An aetheric sapphire set into a silver band.

The other sensors continued collecting data while James set the cameras to create a high-resolution photomosaic of the whole planet.

The hard part of the work was soon done, and there was only one thing left to do. He unzipped a pocket in the arm of his suit and pulled out a small bronze-coloured pin-badge. It was a stylised griffin with wings outstretched, its metal gleaming in the cockpit light. With a smile, he held it aloft and let go, allowing it to float freely. A light tap set it spinning slowly.

It had belonged to his father; he'd won it when James

was a child. His father had completed a space-themed videogame and sent off in the post for his prize: this small badge featuring the game's emblem. It was a game James and his father had bonded over.

After Austin had told James he was going to Neptune, his thoughts immediately went to his father. The pin-badge was worn and a bit battered in places; James normally kept it attached to his suitcase. It was only after he'd started training and the idea of Neptune set in that he even thought about it. He soon came up with a plan, but he knew he wouldn't have been allowed to do it if he'd asked. So he told no-one, not even Angela.

He clambered out of his seat then floated to the rear of the cockpit and opened the hatch. Sitting in the centre of the cargo bay was a small box securely fastened to the ship's folded robotic arm. The monitoring satellite was only around the size of a large suitcase, but it contained an array of advanced equipment and a deployable solar panel. The satellite was to be inserted into Neptunian orbit and left behind for ongoing observations. Floating over to it, he tucked the pin-badge into a tiny opening in the satellite's frame, making sure it couldn't come loose. Then, he retreated back to the cockpit.

The badge weighed next-to-nothing. The addition of its mass to the satellite would have no appreciable effect on its ability to carry out its work; he'd already figured out its impact on the satellite's propellant. It was expected to remain out here in orbit for the next twenty to thirty years, but those were conservative timeframes. So many of these spacecraft continued well past their rated lifetimes. Even with the extra mass, it would still have enough fuel to last far beyond the end of its mission. No-one else would know it was out here, but it would forever hold special meaning for James.

A few button presses later, and the satellite switched on. James extended the *Aurora*'s robotic arm out of the bay and released the little box. As soon as the screen showed it was clear of the arm, the solar panel unfolded and its miniature thrusters fired, orienting its instruments towards the planet. The solar panel rotated on its axis to gather what little light it could to supplement the internal battery.

He made one final check of the satellite's telemetry and closed the bay.

Minutes later, the forward sensor array was also housed back under the *Aurora*'s nose-cone. The ship's reaction-control system turned it away from the planet.

Once more looking into the depths of open space, James moved the ship away from the satellite and through progressively higher orbits.

As the craft heaved itself out from the gravity well of the Ice Giant, James made his final transmission to Earth, warning them to expect his imminent arrival and reminding them to stick the kettle on.

The *Aurora* climbed for a further two hours using its ion drives. James then turned the ship back onto its tangential course and set the throttle control to neutral. He spared one last glance out of the side window at the planet.

All that time moving away, and it doesn't look any smaller. Farewell, Neptune... bye, dad.

He flicked the switch. The drive motors powered up and he set the Austinium drive to spool. The moment it was ready, with a wide smile he slammed the throttle open. This time around he knew what to expect and allowed himself to savour the moment.

But nothing happened.

The grin faded from his face and he glanced around the cockpit. Then, there was a crackle of electricity and the power went out, plunging the *Aurora* into darkness and silence.

Shit.

A second later, the emergency batteries kicked in and dim lights illuminated the cockpit. There was enough power in the batteries to be able to send a transmission.

James opened a channel and said, 'Mission Control, this is the *Aurora*, scratch that last message, something's wrong. I have experienced a total system failure. I am now running on battery power. Stand by.'

He flicked switches all around the cockpit trying to get the main power back on, but all he succeeded in doing was turning the emergency lights off and on. With a slump, he gazed out at the darkness.

The simulations didn't cover this either. What could have caused a total power failure? Think, James...

In his head he replayed the sequence of events that led to the outage. Anxious thoughts intruded. Oxygen was a limited and precious resource; he had more than enough for the mission—the electrolysis system took care of that, taking breathable air from the water tanks—but it would run out eventually. His heart raced at the thought of suffocating out here where no-one could get to him.

Wait a minute... What am I even doing? Here I am worrying about running out of air and I totally forgot I don't actually need it!

It had been many years since the experiments in

TELOMER Labs. There, he had discovered his augmentation allowed him to survive in a vacuum almost indefinitely. It had been a mere intellectual curiosity at the time, overshadowed by more pressing concerns, like holding together his relationship with Angela, and Dr Hales's descent into madness.

He calmed his breathing. So the life support was a non-issue, but what if he couldn't get the power back? He may not suffocate, but he'd be stuck out here for the rest of his immortal life.

If I'm going to get myself home I need to figure out what the problem is and the best way to do that is to go through methodically.

He tried a few switches again to no avail.

Can't fix it from in here.

This time, without the distraction, he thought through what he had done. He'd pulled the *Aurora* away from the planet under normal propulsion, and he hadn't noticed anything amiss. Then he'd initiated the start-up sequence for the jump to FTL. No unusual noises or behaviours there until he opened the throttle.

James leaned forwards and hit the broadcast switch. 'Mission Control, this is the *Aurora*. I'm thinking it might be a malfunction with the FTL drive unit. Best case scenario is it's drawn too much power and triggered some kind of safety switch.

'I've got nothing here in the cockpit; I'm gonna have to go out back and open it up.' He sighed and rubbed his face with the back of his hand. 'Honestly praying it doesn't take too long to fix. I didn't quite reach escape velocity—didn't think I'd need to. But now everything's shut down... Eventually I'll curve back around and start falling towards the planet. I haven't done the calculations, but I reckon my orbit will be pretty extreme. *Aurora* out.'

The cargo bay was pressurised and sealed against the vacuum of space, doors closed and locked, but James had his helmet and gloves back on all the same. Maybe it was a comfort thing, but if something else went wrong he didn't fancy staring out at the naked sky with nothing between his skin and the cold void, no matter the fact he'd probably survive it.

James had a tough time squeezing his way through the cramped bay, past the folded robotic arm which took up most of the room, and around bolted-down boxes and other compartments. The spaceplane was a few metres shorter than the old STS shuttles of the eighties and it carried a lot more junk in its trunk. So there was a lot of equipment and not a lot of room. It didn't help that Austin's team hadn't optimised it either. Of course, this was only a test flight with a few cheeky extra activities shoved in for economy, not a full-fledged mission. No-one would have expected James to actually have to get through the mess and access any important components. They had, at least, had the good sense to put some tools in for him.

He reached the back wall and unbolted the rectangular panel near the top, allowing it to float away freely for a moment before he grabbed it and secured it down by jamming it between a couple of exposed pipes. Then, he reached into the opening where the Austinium drive lived. The pressure difference of his suited marshmallow arm going into the hole wafted thin white wisps of trailing smoke out from around his sleeve.

Wait a minute...

He retracted his helmet and was hit immediately by the acrid smell of burnt electronics. His heart sank.

Shit. That's going to be a problem.

It took him over an hour to pull all of the destroyed components out of the small compartment, some of which he could only guess as to their purpose. He'd been given a crash course in the working of the drive unit during his short training, but an electrical engineer, he was not. His base knowledge of the physics involved helped get him up to speed, but the application skirted the bleeding edge of what anyone thought was even possible. So it was a challenge, to say the least. That meant there was no time for him to become intimately familiar with the complex array of electronics that went into the thing.

All the while, he cursed whoever was responsible for creating such a tiny access hatch for so large a device. Groping around in a nearby toolbox, he found a torch, which he then shone into the hole. It looked like whatever had happened had been confined to the immediate area. Aside from a bit of superficial discolouration from the heat on its outer casing, the Austinium generator further towards the back of the tiny cubbyhole looked relatively unscathed. A positive, all things considered.

Hallelujah. I dread to think what I'd have to do to fix that thing. At least with these boards I might have a fighting chance, assuming there's something I can scavenge for parts.

He soaked up the sweat from his forehead with a flannel from the tool kit and made his way back to the cockpit. Without bothering to seat himself, he gave an update for Mission Control.

Before long, he was back in the cargo bay pulling out

one crate after another, opening them and searching through. Another couple of hours passed and he found nothing that looked like it would be of any use.

With screwdriver in hand, he eyed up the robotic arm. Perhaps there was something compatible in there? The arm had already done its job, after all.

He stopped himself.

On second thought, I'd better wait for their response. If I start pulling random stuff apart looking for replacement parts, I could cause more damage. The Captain will know what's wrong.

Grabbing the floating pieces of burnt parts, he headed back to the cockpit, then strapped himself in and started to examine them.

At first glance they looked exactly how he'd expect scorched silicon to look. Clearly this wasn't the work of a safety switch, but it did seem to support the theory that something had drawn too much power and busted them.

But the more he stared, the less sense that made. The marks; the way in which they were burnt, with streaks and patterning, suggested something external to the components had exploded and caused the damage. There were also some metal shards that didn't look like they belonged.

He leaned forward and pressed the broadcast button. 'Mission Control, I'm just having a look at these boards and something seems a bit off. I think something exploded in the cavity, judging by the look of these scorch marks. I've got some bits here that could have been part of the component that went bang. Any of that make sense to you? Over.'

He sat back, giving the board a little flick which set

it spinning, and he frowned. Then, something flashed out of the corner of his eye which made him glance up at the window.

What the...?

He pulled himself closer to the window and stared. Seconds later something small streaked past from left to right, and then another.

James's eyes widened and a pit formed in his stomach when it dawned on him what was happening. Looking out of the port side window, he could see the rings of Neptune spread out wide, appearing much larger than when he'd last seen them.

Without the sensors, it had completely escaped James's notice that the ship had passed aphelion and was now falling sidewards at orbital speed, grazing the edge of a sparse halo of debris above the rings. And every mote was a bullet.

Fucking marvellous.

Some quick and dirty calculations showed he had less than ten hours until the *Aurora* would pass through the ring. But as he descended, the density of the halo would increase, and so too would the chance of a catastrophic impact.

It would leave things with Mission Control extraordinarily close. They would receive the first of his transmissions soon, but it would be a further two hours before they knew anything had gone wrong. All told, it could be eight hours or more before he received a solution from them, and by that time the ship—and his body—could be riddled with holes.

Vacuum I can survive, but that'll certainly kill me. I'm not indestructible like Captain Scarlet! What did

Dr Hales call it? 'Biological immortality'? Like a lobster or something.

As if to punctuate his thoughts, two dull thuds sounded behind him, coming from the cargo bay. He scrambled out of the seat, following the faint whistle of rushing air. Without hesitation he grabbed the repair kit from the tool box. The tiny holes were on opposite sides of the fuselage, indicating a single micrometeorite had passed straight through. No alarm sounded. The spaceplane had come equipped with internal low-pressure sensors, but due to the power failure, they were inoperable.

James floated over to the starboard puncture and pulled a roll of black tape and some resin out from the repair kit. Once patched, he repeated the procedure on the port side and the whistling stopped.

Floating free, he sighed, then secured the repair kit to his suit. It was only a matter of time before more holes appeared, and he figured he'd need the tape and resin quick to hand.

There's no way I can wait for Austin's help now. I'll have to fix this myself.

CHAPTER EIGHT
Repairs

JUBILATION TURNED TO DESPAIR at Mission Control as the messages from the *Aurora* filtered through over the course of a few hours, each one bringing worse news than the last. What had been a tangible release of tension for Angela morphed into palpitations and a churning stomach.

She watched on, standing outside the plexiglass door to one of the centre's meeting rooms, her nails biting into her folded arms as Austin debated with a whole team of scientists and engineers. It wasn't fair. She'd only just got James back, and now it seemed she was listening to him die slowly. Each message could be the last she would ever hear from him.

The director ordered Austin to hold off making a response when the first troubling transmission came in, reasoning that James would try to determine more about the problem. He was right. As the messages poured in, the severity of the situation became clear, their worst fears realised: The *Aurora* had been sabotaged. Austin made it plain there was absolutely nothing inside the drive unit's cavity that could have exploded, aside from the Austinium generator itself.

Elsewhere, flight controllers performed trajectory calculations based on the ship's last known position. They quickly came to the conclusion that James was going to skim one of the planet's rings. His odds of survival were slim, and diminishing with each passing hour.

The whys and wherefores and other questions about the sabotage remained a mystery, but for now they had given way to the more pressing conundrum: how to fix the ship.

Angela wasn't an engineer. She had no knowledge, experience or insight to share. Her head swam and feet dragged from the lack of sleep. The feeling of utter powerlessness rankled her.

As she stared sightlessly at the pane, her thoughts turned to the sabotage.

Why would someone do such a thing? No... that's a stupid question.

Coming up with a motive was easy, they had already run through several when they thought the *Aurora* destroyed. The ISA had enemies aplenty. She'd gleaned as much from the director's press conference. From the increasingly militant groups subscribed to Guy Furious's anti-space philosophy, to the growing contingent of disgruntled alien-worshippers, all had a bone to pick with the worldwide space programme.

The better question is 'how?'

How could someone get so far as to gain access to the

Aurora's internal systems and plant an explosive? Why not destroy the spaceplane entirely on the first drive activation? Why not do it on the runway, for that matter? Why wait until James was about to return home to fry the ship's systems?

'You look deep in thought,' said Ilona as she sidled up to Angela.

'I'm worried.'

Ilona shook her head. 'That's not it. You were worried earlier. But right now? There's something else on your mind.'

Angela looked sidelong at her. 'And how would you know that? We've only just met; you barely know me at all.'

'I'm observant, is all. Always been good with body language.'

'Well, you're right,' said Angela, her jaw set. 'If you're that intuitive maybe you can help me figure this out. Austin is certain someone's tampered with the *Aurora*. But... Why do it this way? There's three options I can come up with. One: they wanted the ship as far away as possible so the prototype couldn't ever be recovered—'

'But if they didn't want anyone to have the drive, outright destroying it would have had the same effect.'

'Yes, unless they couldn't build a powerful enough explosive that would fit in the cavity, so rigged it to short everything out instead when it was irrecoverable.'

Ilona looked upwards and bit her lip, then said, 'All right, what's option two?'

'Option two is that they wanted to make it look like the drive was unreliable, like there'd been an accident. The death of an astronaut would halt the project.'

'Unlikely. Three?'

'Occam's Razor: They made a mistake. They wanted to make it look like the test failed but didn't want to kill anyone. It was meant to short out the drive before the ship left Earth but something went wrong and it didn't activate until the second time around.'

'That one is certainly possible, but I think there's a simpler solution to satisfy Occam's Razor,' said Ilona with a smirk. 'Option four: They were waiting to see if the drive worked first.'

Angela snorted. 'How is that simpler?'

Ilona shrugged and leaned with her hand against the plexiglass. 'If the drive failed or blew itself up, there'd be no need for the sabotage at all and they wouldn't have a death on their conscience. I mean, they haven't killed anyone yet, right?'

'I'm not convinced by that.' Angela shook her head and slumped back to the doorframe. 'The time scale means they'd need to know or at least get an idea that the drive works before they manually sent a signal to set off the bomb. But if you're right then that means the perpetrator would have to have been here, right in this room.'

Angela's eyes remained fixed on Ilona, but her focus drifted. Puzzle pieces began to fit together in her mind. The saboteur would have needed access to the spacecraft without raising suspicion to plant the explosive, which also suggested someone familiar with its inner workings. As far as Angela had seen, the only people who had been able to go anywhere near the ship on the lead-up to the launch were members of Austin's engineering team. The only problem was that none of those team members had been present in the Mission Control Centre when the idea was first floated that the *Aurora* had made a successful jump.

She conveyed this to Ilona who waved her hand and said, 'There's nothing to say there couldn't have been a second.'

'A second? This is getting far more complicated than you originally suggested. Multiple parties?'

And yet, it makes more sense than the idea of people who have never killed before suddenly turning to murder to make their point.

'It's not that much more complicated,' said Ilona with a glance around the room. 'We've still narrowed down the list of people it could be.' She raised her hand and counted them out on her fingers. 'Just Captain Queen's team, and the flight controllers who were here when we received confirmation from LIGO.'

'Not just the flight controllers,' said Angela. She cast her mind back to those excruciating hours when they were still awaiting James's first transmission. There were a handful of staff members, herself, Austin and Ilona, and… someone else. 'There was also that young journalist snoozing in the corner the whole time. Little weasel trying to get the big scoop. He's the most out-of-place.'

'So we start with him.'

'What?'

'He's still here; let's go ask him.'

Angela scoffed. 'Ask him what? If he's the saboteur? Like, "Oh excuse me sir, did you happen to put a bomb in my husband's spaceship?" Come off it.'

Ilona opened her mouth to respond, but Austin

pushed the door and stepped through, rubbing the back of his neck.

He acknowledged Ilona then put a hand on Angela's arm and spoke fast. 'We think we've got a solution. Jimmy can still fix the *Aurora*, but he ain't gonna have a lot of time.'

'What does he need to do?' said Angela.

Austin motioned to her to follow him and started off towards his computer terminal, weaving around the desks as he went. He moved nimbly for a man of his age, and Angela had to skip a little to keep up.

On reaching his work-station, he said, 'There's a lot of redundancies on that ship.'

'Is that unusual?'

'Not when it comes to crewed spaceflight, no. In simple terms, he just needs to grab a couple of spare cables and run them from one board to another to bypass the broken ones. Based on what he's told us about the problem, or rather, what he's not told us, we think we know which boards are fucked.'

'And that's good?'

Austin chuckled as he tapped away at his keyboard, putting his message into text form. 'He's one lucky son-of-a-bitch, I'll tell you that much. This workaround ain't gonna be as good as what was originally there, but it's a choice between a ninety-nine-point-nine percent reliability rating and an eighty-seven percent one, so it should be good enough to get him home at least.

'The biggest problem with it all is time. He won't get the instructions for the next four hours, and that's cutting it real tight. Best case scenario, Jimmy figures it out on his own way before he gets this.'

With the message complete, Austin tapped the enter key triumphantly and stepped back from the desk. 'Now, we wait.'

Angela spared a glance towards Ilona, who had remained at the meeting room entrance and was now in discussion with the engineers from Austin's team.

I hope she doesn't let slip about our suspicions. I'd better bring Austin into the loop.

'Hey,' Angela started in a low voice, 'I've been thinking about this sabotage business. Ilona and I are concerned a member of your team might be involved.'

Austin fixed Angela with a freezing stare behind an inscrutable expression. Then he motioned for her to lean in closer. In her ear, he whispered, 'I think so, too. I didn't want you to get involved in this, but I have a suspect in mind. The only problem is—'

'They weren't here to know about the *Aurora*'s success,' Angela interjected. 'I know. Ilona and I are confident someone else in this room sent the transmission to set off the explosive.'

Austin shook his head and scratched at his beard. 'Transmission can't have come from here, I'd have noticed. It'll be in the logs, too. But they'll have needed equipment just like ours to do it.'

'Then that person in here was probably in contact with someone off-site. A fly on the wall. Watching. Keeping their bosses apprised of the situation.'

Austin and Angela stared at one another for a long moment. Then, Austin's eyes brightened and he clicked his fingers.

'The journalist!' they said in unison.

* * *

'Argh! Fucking piece of shit.' James cried, lobbing a circuit board across the cargo bay.

He sat floating with his legs and arms crossed and a scowl on his face, surrounded by tumbling computer components, wires, screws, and the gutted corpse of the *Aurora*'s robotic arm.

Nothing fits. There's not one goddamn component in here that can replace the burnt stuff.

Holes patched with black tape peppered the cargo bay. Several micrometeorites had punched through in the final few hours of the long wait, which James diligently repaired while making sporadic progress taking apart the cargo arm. And it had been a long wait indeed. The five hours before, he'd turned the place upside-down looking for something to fix the ship, stopping to eat some of his rations and relieve himself in between. All he'd found were ribbon cables, but no spare boards. The cargo arm had been his last resort; a total shot-in-the-dark.

Now he glanced about the bay looking for anything else he may have missed—perhaps another computerised victim—allowing the odd oath to escape under his breath.

Why aren't there any redundancies for this sort of thing? Most important part of the ship and it has no backup?

His mind went back to the NASA shuttles. They had backups for every key system. How could Austin have missed this sort of thing? How could the ISA have let the *Aurora* get through its orbital tests without them? The ship was smaller, naturally lighter and mechanically simpler than those previous designs, after all.

No, Austin wouldn't have neglected something so vital.

Even the *Magnum Opus*'s re-entry vehicle had plenty of redundant systems.

I must be missing something...

A frown crossed his face and he twisted to look at the open hatch. With a push off the floor, he drifted over, bringing himself to a halt with hands splayed either side of the opening. He grabbed the torch floating nearby and surveyed the remaining boards inside for what felt like the umpteenth time, not knowing what he expected to find.

The extra scrutiny paid off.

'Oh for fuck's sake,' James muttered. He closed his eyes with a sigh and rested his head on the frame.

To the far edge of two of the boards was an oblong of black plastic. Where they jutted out from the surface of the boards, the viewing angle was too extreme to be able to see the tops, but James recognised them as ports for ribbon cables.

The radio in the cockpit crackled.

James shoved off and floated across the bay, back through the doorway.

Eh? No audio?

The screen flashed with text and James scanned Austin's message. Out of the corner of his eye, the Neptunian rings loomed large in the window. With only two hours to go until impact, the one ring segment now filled the view entirely.

James wiped his face with his bare hand. 'Such a simple solution. If I'd have known about this from the start I could've been home by now.'

With all haste, he moved back to the cargo bay and located the spare ribbon cables. Then, reaching into the access hatch, he fumbled about trying to line up the connectors with their corresponding ports.

A satisfying click told him one end of the first cable was connected. As he trailed his fingers along to the other end, a dull thud sounded behind him, accompanied by the infernal whistle of escaping air.

Then another.

And another.

James closed his eyes and steadied his breathing. Getting these cables connected was the priority. The longer the *Aurora* stayed on its course, the more danger he was in. It was a small mercy no rock fragment had yet penetrated the Austinium generator.

Remaining at the hatch, he clicked the other end of the first cable in place and moved onto the second.

Another two impacts came from the cockpit, one of which sounded like it had gone through a window.

The second cable proved trickier than the first. James pushed down on the connector, but it was around the wrong way. With just the one hand and his arm fully outstretched, he painstakingly turned the cable over in his fingers.

There was another thud immediately to his right. Something brushed against James's suit and punched its way through the other side of the ship. James's heart felt like it skipped a beat.

That was close.

As he reached further to plug in the cable, a searing pain shot through his abdomen and he fumbled.

The edges of his vision darkened. He pulled his arm out of the hatch and looked down at his side.

Globules of blood pooled around a hole in the side of his suit.

'Damn it.'

* * *

Four hours had passed at Mission Control. Angela and Austin—accompanied by Ilona—presented their suspicions to Dr Azzopardi, who quietly ordered a lockdown of the facility. Angela had stood by the director's side as he gathered the staff together. Flight controllers and engineers and service personnel; even the young journalist came in close to hear the director's words.

Against Austin's recommendation, but with Angela's support and Ilona's keen eyes, Dr Azzopardi told them of the likely presence of the saboteur (or saboteurs) among them. Amid gasps and a rising thrum of discontent, he announced that they would be interviewing everyone, each in turn.

Angela leaned across to Ilona. 'See anything?' she said, her voice hoarse and her eyelids heavy.

Ilona simply shook her head. Not a single suspect had stirred under her watchful gaze. They had hoped the abrupt announcement would draw out at least one of the saboteurs, sending them into a panic about being discovered.

'Damn. Ah well, Plan B it is,' said Angela through a groan.

The interviews had taken much longer than expected. Dr Azzopardi insisted on ruling out the flight controllers first so they could return to their work monitoring the *Aurora*'s situation. The director was satisfied the cohort had no knowledge of the sabotage beyond what had already been revealed to them. And now, after the time had passed by which James should have received Austin's instructions, they finally moved onto the Captain's team of engineers.

Angela stood outside the same meeting room as before, watching Austin grill each of his staff. With the door closed she could hear nothing, but the faces of the engineers told the whole story. Some reeled at the accusations, their faces red as they shouted back and slammed their palms on the table. Others sat straight, with their heads held high, talking simply and calmly. Yet, eventually, all faltered under Austin's interrogation.

The Captain was good, very good. He moved around the room, applying and easing pressure in all the right places. His military background was plain as day and even made Angela feel a little intimidated.

She knew from previous conversations over the last few months that he'd done his share of interrogations during his service. Along with chewing out his subordinates, it was a part of the job he'd hated, but one he excelled at nonetheless.

With a yawn she stepped away from the door. Her mind fogged, and in the low light of the Mission Control Centre it was a struggle to keep her eyes open. Caffeine had been keeping her going but she was now running on fumes.

'You should get some sleep,' said Ilona as she came out of the meeting room. 'Go back to your dorm and we can let you know when there's an update.'

'I can sleep when I'm dead,' said Angela. Her tone was sharper than she intended and she sighed. 'I just need to clear my head a bit, I'm going for a walk.'

Breathing in the chill night air, Angela sighed and leant against the wall with her eyes closed. Despite the lockdown, this little enclosed courtyard remained open. The outer walls were high and lined with razor wire, with only the one door back into the building. The climate control inside had dried out her airways, so despite the cold, being outside felt refreshing.

The stark brutalism of the courtyard reminded her of her secondary school days when she and her friends used to sneak a quick smoke around the back of the bike sheds to decompress from the various dramas of teenage life. Though she had no desire to pick up the habit again—she'd dropped it soon after starting college and hadn't had a craving in decades—she found herself yearning for those simpler times.

She opened her eyes and stared at the clear sky. Only the brightest stars were visible through the light pollution. Even though she had no idea where Neptune was, Angela couldn't help but pretend she was looking straight at James.

I'm going to find whoever did this to you and—

Too exhausted to finish the thought, Angela slid down the wall and sat on the floor, resting her head on her knees. Drowsiness began to take her, and her mind emptied as sleep took hold.

There was a muttering on the wind.

Angela's eyes shot open and she peered around, her ears pricked. It hadn't been a trick of the mind. There was definitely a voice, carried by the wind from her right.

After easing herself up from the ground—a painful prospect that made her regret getting down there in the first place—she crept along the wall.

The voice grew louder. It was male, agitated, almost panicked, and she recognised it.

She poked her head around the corner. There was a man in the shadows smoking, chattering on his phone. By his manner of dress, it looked to be one of the people from Austin's team: the Hungarian quantum field researcher.

'No, no, they don't suspect—' he said, gesticulating wildly. 'Look, the plan failed and the ship survived, you need to accept—What? How was I supposed to know it would misfire? Your people built the damn thing. Amateurs. I upheld my end of the deal, now you make good on yours and release my family.'

Angela sucked in a breath.

So this is the saboteur!

The call ended and the researcher looked at the screen with wide eyes. He jabbed at the screen and held the phone to his ear.

'Shit, shit, shit,' he hissed, then put the phone away and shoved his hands into his pockets.

As he rushed towards Angela's position, she emerged. Before he could react, she gripped him by the shoulders and slammed him against the wall.

Cries of shock and confusion echoed in the night as the man struggled under her grasp. A look of recognition came over him and he stopped and said, 'Mrs Fowler? What—what're you doing out here? Let go of me!'

'You slimy bastard,' she said, her mouth contorting into a snarl. 'What did you do to the *Aurora*?'

'What? I have no idea what you're talking about.'

'Don't give me that bullshit, I heard every single word, you great thundering prat.'

The door flew open behind them with a crash. The commotion had echoed in the stillness and drawn attention. Austin and Dr Azzopardi rushed around the corner and skidded to a halt.

'Get this crazy woman off of me!' cried the man, entreating the director with a pained expression.

Angela pinned him harder to the wall, and he yelped. 'He's the saboteur,' she said. 'I overheard him talking with someone—'

'It's not like that. Director, please, I can explain everything!'

A guttural roar escaped Angela, and her heartbeat pounded in her ears. She slammed the researcher against the wall again.

The director stepped forwards and placed a hand on Angela's shoulder. 'Mrs Fowler, I know things have been difficult but assaulting my staff isn't the way to handle it.'

She shook the director off and came up close to the researcher's face. 'Whatever you've got to say had better be the truth or so help me god…'

'Angie,' Austin said. His voice was loud and firm, then softened quickly. 'Let me take it from here. He's the last one to interview anyway.'

With a huff, Angela released the man and paced back and forth flexing her hands.

The man looked between the three of them.

'Well?' said Austin. 'Start 'splainin', boy.'

The engineer stuttered and huffed and puffed, then sighed and began in a low voice, 'It's true. I set the charge. But I had no choice, they took my family.'

'Who's "they?"' said Angela, stopping in her tracks.

'Anti-spacers, Guy Furious's supporters. Hardliners. They tracked me down and gave me an explosive device to rig inside the *Aurora* before launch. They said if I did my part, they'd release my family, and if I involved the authorities in any way, they'd...' His voice faltered into a sob. 'I told them when I'd done it, but they changed the deal. I argued with them but it was useless, they said I'd get my wife and kids back after the bomb went off. They wanted to—'

'To wait to see if the drive worked before using it, right?' said Angela.

The engineer tilted his head. 'No? They wanted to blow up the ship. They thought if they could make the drive out to be unreliable and deadly, that we'd shut down the entire project.'

'Wait, what?'

'But something went wrong,' the man continued, 'neither the ship, nor the Commander, were supposed to survive. The bomb must have misfired. Shoddy workmanship, by the sound of it. Now they're blaming me!'

Angela faltered. It didn't make any sense; it didn't track with their investigation. How could she and Ilona have been so wrong? Did this mean there was no second saboteur?

Austin removed his glasses, pinched the bridge of his nose and groaned. 'So who were you talkin' to on the phone?'

'They set someone to keep an eye on me here to make sure I didn't say anything. Someone who could be in the Mission Control room and report back to them...'

Angela pursed her lips.

So there is *a second!*

Austin shook his head. 'I've already interrogated the journalist. Kid's got nothing, a real wet blanket. I'm not buying your story.'

'That journalist kid? What are you talking about?' The

researcher ran his hands through his fluffy light-brown hair. 'No, no, the contact was a woman.'

Angela raised an eyebrow and shared a sidelong look with Austin.

'There's lots of women here,' said Austin. 'How about you give us a name?'

The researcher's cheeks flushed and he said, 'I never met her in person, I don't know who she is. But she was supposed to be one of the flight controllers, I think.'

Dr Azzopardi frowned. 'Impossible, we have already investigated all of the flight controllers.'

Turning to the director, the Captain sighed and rolled his shoulders. 'All except one.'

Angela's heart sank as she spoke aloud: 'Ilona.'

CHAPTER NINE
Back in Time for Tea

The pain pulsed through James's side as he pressed the heel of his palm against the entry wound. It had been a lucky shot, all things considered. The micrometeorite had barely passed through his flank, shallow enough to have missed organs, but deep enough to still be problematic.

Gasping and groaning through the pain, James scanned the bay for something to patch himself up with. His thoughts went at first to the tape and resin attached to his suit, but quickly dismissed it as a terrible idea. His abdomen was not, after all, a fuselage.

His eyes fell on a first aid kit in the far corner. There was nothing for it, he would have to push off from the wall to get to it.

Every movement was excruciating as he manoeuvred himself into position. He'd never truly appreciated how much he used that set of muscles until now. With a light tap of his feet, he drifted along the length of the short bay and stopped himself against the wall.

Reaching down with his free hand, he scooped up the kit box. Inside was gauze, sterilising wipes and surgical tape, and so he set about wrapping himself. It was a bodge job but at least he now had the freedom of both his hands. Thinking back on his past injuries, he knew his augmentation ought to be able to stem the blood flow relatively quickly. It was just a case of giving it a chance to work. But what effect would microgravity have on his ability to heal? For an ordinary human, wounds don't heal well in space; would the same hold true for him?

If I can get full power back, I can run the drive for a while and stand against the wall. If I can simulate even a bit of gravity with acceleration…

No matter what, getting the power back on remained the top priority. It was only a matter of time before another chunk of rock shot through, and he may not be so lucky the next time.

Wincing with the pain, he pushed himself back to the access hatch. With the light of his torch, he peered inside. The cable floated freely within the cavity. He'd been struck before he could clip it into place, and the shock had made him let go carelessly. As a result, the cable was further back than he'd anticipated. It still looked within arm's reach, but it would be a painful stretch.

James fed his arm into the hole. There wasn't enough space for him to look and reach at once. He had to creep his fingers forwards. If he knocked the cable too hard, he could send it flying to the back of the space where he couldn't reach.

His jaw hurt from clenching his teeth and his heart

ached as he stretched his arm out to its full length without finding anything. After a long moment the palp-like motion of his fingers brushed against something which seemed to tumble away into oblivion. He groped some more, finding nothing but air.

With a sudden shot of adrenaline and a gasp of searing pain, he lunged as hard as he could with his open hand, clamping it shut in pure faith.

The cable was his, caught in his desperate grasp.

James breathed out slowly as he drew out the cable, and clutched it to his chest. The pain subsided as he relaxed within his suit. He took a moment to catch his breath, then reached up again and clicked both ends of the cable into place.

Holes still remained in the cargo bay, with air gradually escaping. For a moment, James considered taking the time to patch them, but when he looked down at his injury to see the dressing barely containing his blood, he thought better of it.

Seated in the cockpit once again, he held out his hand to the controls and muttered a plea, a prayer, or perhaps both; he wasn't sure. Then with baited breath he flicked the switches.

The lights and power came back on as though nothing had gone wrong; his diligence rewarded.

Through a pained sigh he said, 'Thank fuck for that,' and immediately fired the RCS thrusters. The field of stars beyond the window streaked across his vision and came to a halt as the *Aurora* turned on its axis, opposing its deadly trajectory.

Without further hesitation, he set a timed burn, threw the throttle open and clambered out of the seat. The acceleration was gradual enough for him to fall lightly against the back wall of the cargo bay, but he felt himself become heavier as more time went by.

The *Aurora*'s Achelon-inspired ion drives were not capable of producing 1G of thrust for more than a few minutes, but that's all James's augmented body needed. The bleeding had slowed considerably thanks to the dressing working in concert with his augmentation, so most of the work was done. A couple of minutes simulating Earth-like gravity should do the trick and allow James to ride home without the risk of bleeding out.

He savoured the time his world had an up and down again. Feet astride the access hatch which he had not yet closed, he stood still and waited as the spaceplane accelerated away from the Neptunian rings and their deadly halo.

All too soon, the burn came to an end and the world regained its omnidirectionality. James examined his wound, gingerly removing the dressing, and found it no longer bleeding. It was far from healed, but at least he would survive the return trip. He spent some time finally patching the remaining holes in the cargo bay and the couple in the cockpit. Oxygen levels were low, but it was of little concern. Another two hours and he'd be back home safe and sound.

Secured back in his seat, he allowed himself a moment's rest and reflection. Austin's last message had contained only a solution, he still had no idea how or why anything had gone wrong with the ship. He thought back to the scorch marks and extra pieces; could someone have tampered with the *Aurora*? He'd warned Dr Azzopardi against going public because of exactly this kind of thing.

But for someone to get close enough to have access to the inside of the ship? Staying silent wouldn't have made a difference.

The anti-space movement Guy Furious started years ago had been in equal parts insidious and ridiculous. There was just enough truth to his original ravings to sow seeds of distrust in the global space programme. NASA and the ESA's post-Mars actions certainly didn't help matters. No matter what he said on TV, how many times he condemned the violent actions of his hardline supporters, the movement had grown beyond him. A new reality for the ISA was emerging. The previous bombing was clearly not a one-off incident, but something they would have to contend with in alarming regularity. James had averted his own tragedy out here, but was this a mere portent of things to come?

He thought of Angela. She must have been worried sick, but he knew she wouldn't have sat around. He smiled inwardly, imagining all the kinds of hell she'd have raised.

God help anyone at Mission Control who got in her way.

With a flick of the plaid switch, the drive motors powered up. James set the drive to spool. He prayed again that his repair work would hold out. Then, suppressing his anxiety, he slammed the throttle open.

The stars ahead stretched out to breaking point, and with a crack the ship lurched away towards home.

* * *

Angela waited, pacing back and forth while Austin threw the quantum field researcher into the interview room and locked the door behind him.

She was wide awake now, all tiredness overtaken by the swirling mix of emotions. The anger was raw and painful: the heartache of betrayal. More than that, she felt a fool; she had trusted Ilona, counted her a friend. How could she have been so easily led up the garden path? It all became clear to her: why Ilona had been so desperate to push her towards the journalist, and why she had manoeuvred her way into being one of the investigators. It must have been to keep suspicion off herself as long as possible after everything went tits up. Now they needed to find her.

'She won't have left,' said Austin, leaning against the door. 'Remember, this whole place is locked down tight, and so far, she doesn't know we know.'

Angela stared out into the rows of staffed computer terminals. The flight controllers were tapping and clicking, watching and waiting, and conversing among themselves as the data from the stricken spacecraft poured in. In the diagram on the large screen, the marker for the *Aurora* edged closer to Neptune's rings. If Austin's solution failed, James would be lost forever, all because of Ilona. And the chances were they wouldn't know whether it worked until either James turned up back home, or they lost telemetry.

When Angela finally spoke, her jaw was stiff from grinding her teeth. 'I can't believe I fell for it. If only I'd seen it sooner,'

Austin shook his head. He sounded just as tired as Angela had felt earlier. Far from re-energising him, this new revelation just seemed to weary him further. 'There was nothing to see. She had us all going, don't beat yourself up over it.'

'That's not entirely true,' said the director as he approached from behind Austin, now accompanied by Lieutenant Colonel Dryden. 'I should have seen something was wrong. I have had trouble with Ilona on and off in the past, ever since her boyfriend died in that accident.'

'You mean girlfriend, right?' said Angela with a frown.

The director returned her expression and folded his arms. 'No, her boyfriend was a test pilot for us on one of the early *Aurora* prototypes. There was an accident and he died. I... thought she had come to terms with it.'

'Wait, no, she told me her girlfriend was killed during a break-in at home.'

'I've never heard that story,' said Austin with a troubled look on his face. 'As far as I know, her ex-girlfriend is still very much alive. Moved out of town a year after Ilona joined us here. When she offered to help you, I thought she would talk about the accident.'

Angela kissed her teeth. 'That duplicitous bitch. She lied to distance herself from it, to cover up her motive.'

'So how do we want to play this?' Austin asked in a low voice. 'Here she comes now.'

Following his gaze, Angela looked to the far end of the room. Ilona marched around the edge of the Mission Control Centre, a stack of papers in her arms, as the main doors crept closed behind her.

Angela's heart raced. There was no time to think, she'd be with them in seconds.

Barely above a whisper Dryden said, 'Act natural, everyone. Director, we need evidence before we can make a move. Something to give the police when they arrive.'

Dr Azzopardi leaned in close to the colonel. 'You've called them already? Good...'

The director's voice faded from Angela's attention. She stared daggers at the other woman, now fast-approaching.

'Fuck that,' she said, setting off at a march of her own towards Ilona.

'Angie, don't!' Austin cried in a rasp.

She felt a hand attempt to grab her arm, but easily shook it off. It was time to put an end to all this. No more messing around, no wait-and-see, no painstaking evidence gathering. If it meant Angela had to work with Ilona for one more second, playing pretend, she'd snap. Exhausted, running on adrenaline, wracked with worry, guilt, anger and regret, she'd already reached her breaking point.

Within a fraction of a second, Angela was face-to-face with Ilona. She gave the woman just enough time—generously, she thought—to look up. Ilona's expression brightened, then turned to horror as Angela's fist barrelled towards her.

Ilona stumbled back, scattering papers everywhere, and cried out, holding her cheek.

Overbalanced from the force of the blow, Angela briefly dropped to her knees. Shaking her reddened fist, she stood again, panting.

'What the fuck's gotten into you?' Ilona said, wincing as she touched her face.

'Don't give me that crap, I know it was you,' Angela roared, pointing at Ilona. 'I know it was you, don't even deny it.'

As she made to lunge at the other woman, Austin and Dryden's arms wrapped around hers, holding her in place.

'Let go of me, Austin.' She yanked her arms against the hold, but they would not budge.

'You got her, Angie, that's enough,' said Austin, struggling against her. 'I know you're angry. Hell, so am I, but we can't just let you beat her to death.'

'The police are on their way, they'll handle this,' said the director. Addressing Ilona, he continued, 'Explain yourself, Illes. We have reason to believe you are the one behind the sabotage of the *Aurora*.'

'What?' Ilona said, her eyes darting from the director to Angela and back. 'No, that's bullshit, sir. I was helping you find the saboteurs. Why would I do that if I were the one?'

'Liar!' Angela yanked even harder against Austin and Dryden's hold, but still they remained firm. 'You've been stringing us along this whole time.'

'But—'

'I know about your boyfriend's accident, you lying bitch,' Angela spat. 'And your ex being alive. All that comforting talk and solidarity, but the very first words out of your mouth to me were a lie.'

'The journalist—'

'A red herring. You were trying to buy yourself time. To pin it on someone else and wait for an opening to get away. But Austin already cleared him, and you're the only one left.'

Ilona stared at Angela agog. After a long moment, still holding her now swelling cheek, her expression relaxed and she laughed.

'What's so fucking funny?'

'You,' she said, steadying herself. 'You figured it out. Yeah I ordered the bomb placed into the *Aurora*. And yeah, I was the mole after all. What a surprise, I bet that hurt, didn't it? Well, *fuck you*. Fuck you, fuck this place, and fuck James Fowler and his stupid fucking spaceplane.'

'You've got nowhere to go, Ilona,' said Austin. 'You can't escape.'

Ilona shrugged. 'Escape? Why bother? I've done my part; I know I can't get out of this place. I had hoped to evade suspicion long enough for you to lift the lockdown, but no matter. My people will have me out soon enough. We're *everywhere*.'

Austin and Dryden released Angela and stepped forward to apprehend Ilona. 'You are coming with us,' said the director, 'and you will make your confession when the police get here.'

Ilona scoffed and looked the director up and down. 'I'm not saying another word.' She fixed her gaze on Angela as Dryden and Austin led her away. '*Sit sidera silere*, bitch.'

Two hours went by. The Hungarian police came soon after Ilona had been locked in the meeting room. The entire time she glared at the researcher sitting across from her, who had on the table in front of him a pen atop a signed confession. After a bit of coaxing and negotiation, Ilona had been convinced to send a message to release the man's family and give up the names of those holding them. Evidently this was in exchange for something, but Angela wasn't privy to the details.

The police had taken statements from everyone, including the journalist, who was unperturbed, and in fact visibly giddy at having had exclusive access to the day's events.

The whole process had taken a while, but eventually the police were confident they had a case they could present. They took Ilona and the quantum field researcher into custody and left.

A gloomy silence hung in the air of the Mission Control Centre as Austin, Angela, Dryden and Dr Azzopardi sat around the table in the meeting room, now released of its function as a makeshift holding cell.

Off in the distance through the room's windows, the big screen still showed the stream of telemetry coming in from the *Aurora*, albeit a blur of colours to Angela's unfocused eyes.

Her mind freed of Ilona, the fog of overwhelming tiredness returned. Her hand ached, knuckles all black and blue and her muscles protested as they tried to release the hours of tension.

It was a while before anybody spoke. 'Sounds like we were right about Ilona's motivations,' said the director, staring at the table with his arms folded. 'A hardline anti-space cell here in Budapest weaponised her grief.'

'Apparently the *rendőrség* have known about them for a while now,' Dryden said, leaning forward and interlinking his fingers. 'I spoke with their commander—the *ezredes*—and they're hoping this will give them an avenue to move against the anti-spacers.'

Angela frowned. 'So what happened with the *Aurora* prototype to cause the accident?'

'Nothing,' said Austin, clearing his throat. 'That was the *IXS-15*. It worked like a dream; sub-orbital of course. Sergeant Myers was a great test pilot. It was an industrial accident with some crates someone hadn't stacked properly. When they fell they caused a head injury and he died a few days later in the hospital.'

Angela tried to muster a despondent expression but

she just felt numb, too drained to respond. But despite everything Ilona had done, Angela's heart still went out to her. A tragic accident putting her in conflict with her employers was one thing, but then to be groomed in her vulnerability by a group of malefactors into carrying out an act of terrorism; it was pitiable.

A perfect cocktail of shit; a whole string of terrible choices and circumstances.

The group fell once again to silence. There was nothing left to do but wait.

After an indeterminate amount of time, a knock on the window disturbed their collective fatigue. A flight controller waved in a frenzy on the other side of the glass.

The director beckoned her in, but instead she opened the door and clung to the frame, shouting, 'The *Aurora*'s back! We're still getting telemetry from when it was at Neptune but now it's being overlaid with a new dataset from geosync, and we have a radio link to the Commander.'

* * *

'Mission Control, this is the *Aurora* checking in from Earth orbit,' said James as the last of the Austinium drive's distortion outside the windows dissipated. 'Altitude three-five-seven-eight-eight, velocity three-point-zero. You'd better be ready with my cuppa, mate. I take it white with one sugar. Over.'

It felt good to be home. Earth shone as bright and blue as ever, with coastlines and clouds and deserts and seas and mountains and flats spread before him in all their wondrous majesty.

After a pause, the radio crackled to life with wild cheering and applause. James winced as the noise peaked through the cockpit's tinny speakers.

It took a while to die down, but when all was calm, Austin's voice, full of relief, came through loud and clear. 'Welcome back, *Aurora*. You're right on time; you had us a little jittery for a while there.'

James smiled, but something seemed off, like Austin was downplaying something. 'It's great to be able to talk to you in real time again. I hope things haven't been too stressful down there?'

The line went quiet for a moment. Then, with a brief stutter Austin replied, 'Yeah, about that... There's a lot to unpack when you get back down here.'

The Captain's words set James on edge. What could have happened to make Austin sound so nervous? More than that, he sounded haggard.

Tentatively, James asked, 'What about Angela? Is... is she alright?'

'Oh yeah dude, she's fine. Everyone's just mighty tired, is all. You can speak to her if you like? (Hey, Angie, come over here, Jimmy wants to know you're alright). Uhh, here she is.'

The line filled with Angela's voice, and they spoke. Angela sounded more exhausted than Austin had indicated, on the verge of tears, even, but her voice was soothing to the soul.

She handed the line back to Austin and James confirmed he was ready to commence the *Aurora*'s orbital transfer.

He was about to fire the thrusters when the Captain stopped him. 'Wait a minute, Jimmy. According to the sensor data, it looks like the ship's sustained some critical damage. We'll need to divert you.'

'Divert?' said James as he removed his hands from the throttle and stick. 'The *Aurora* got hit by a bunch of debris over the rings before I managed to bring the main power back online.'

'Yeah, I can see that from the data. It's damaged the ship's thermal protection. It's not safe to deorbit.'

James shifted in his seat. 'I also got hit by a rock. It's not life-threatening at the moment, but it'll need seeing to sooner rather than later.'

Austin groaned, then said, 'Stand by, *Aurora*.'

James let out a heavy sigh. Of all the things he'd thought about while resting up on the return journey, he hadn't even considered the possibility that the ship might not be safe to land. It was like falling at the final hurdle; so close, so tantalisingly close. Earth was right there. His home, Angela, everyone he ever knew. It couldn't possibly end with him stuck in orbit, could it? At the same time, he couldn't take the risk. Compromised thermal protection meant the ship would disintegrate. He had seen it happen before.

After a while, Austin returned to the radio and James gripped his seat restraints as his stomach fluttered, waiting for the bad news.

'*Aurora*, you are cleared to dock at Skyport Station. They're expecting you, man. Once you've parked her there, you'll be free to take a re-entry capsule for a splashdown. The director's notified the recovery teams. Over.'

James tilted his head back and blew slowly through puffed-out cheeks. The Captain always had a solution. The prospect of seeing the station up close for himself sent a buzz through his body.

He rubbed his face, then said through a grin, 'Copy that, you glorious bastard. Preparing for rendezvous. Over.'

The rendezvous process was long and slow. James flipped the ship so it faced tail-on to its orbital motion and fired the thrusters, bringing the *Aurora* gradually lower. Underneath, the world went by faster and faster as the ship's altitude decreased, bringing it out of geosynchronous and into low-Earth orbit.

After five hours, the Hohmann transfer was complete and, once more facing his direction of travel, James could see the gleaming trunk of Skyport far in the distance. A tiny solitary dot in the blackness, suspended above the glowing limb of the planet.

As the ship approached at its low relative speed, James could make out the shape of the station more easily. Much larger than the International Space Station had been, Skyport made extensive use of new technologies procured from the Achelon wreckage in its construction. It was long and slender, with a rotating habitation ring at one end, to which was affixed an array of glimmering blue solar panels. Off the main cylindrical trunk were other modules and pods, docking ports, cargo containers, radiators and communications antennae.

James couldn't help but smile as he spied a familiar sight attached to one of the berths. A gargantuan, slender spacecraft with two habitation rings, fore and aft. The *Magnum Opus*, dwarfed by the station, sat docked, ready and waiting for its next resupply mission to Arcadia Landing.

Once docked and aboard, aided by one of the station's crew, James said goodbye to the *Aurora* and drifted through the maze of tunnels to a waiting capsule. He watched through one of the tiny windows as the station receded from view, soon swallowed by the encroaching atmospheric haze.

'They'll repair her in no time,' said Austin, munching on his sandwich.

James sat opposite him, snuggled up close to Angela on the picnic bench in the cafeteria garden of the Mission Control Centre. The sun shone bright and hot, uncharacteristic for November in Budapest, but welcome all the same.

'Maybe they should send her down here so the medics can take a look,' said James with a smile. 'They did a bang-up job sorting me out.'

A couple of days had passed since James splashed down in the Pacific, and work was already underway at Skyport to make the *Aurora* safe for re-entry. Austin, Angela, Lieutenant Colonel Dryden and Dr Azzopardi were there waiting for James when he got back to the ISA facility. Angela had thrown her arms around him and sobbed into his chest, and when she peeled herself away, it was Austin's turn, with no fewer tears.

While he recovered from being looked at by the facility's medical staff, the two of them had filled him in on everything that had happened with Ilona and the bomb.

'Hey,' said Angela, looking up at James from his shoulder, 'if I ever start trying to convince you to go back up into space again, just stop me, alright?'

James raised an eyebrow at her. 'How?'

'I dunno.' Angela shrugged. 'Lock me in a cupboard or something, I guess.'

Austin laughed and choked on a bit of his lunch. 'So

is that you done, then Jimmy? No more space?'

James glanced from Angela to Austin and then to the azure sky. After a short pause, he said, 'No, I don't think so. Despite everything, the *Aurora* was incredible. The journey, seeing Neptune and Triton and the rings up close, with my own eyes. There's nothing like it. It was just what I needed, it's… It's reawakened something in me, y'know? Wait, why?'

'Well, there's still plenty of work to do on the *Aurora*,' said Austin, leaning forward on the wood-slatted table. 'Now we know the drive works, it's opening up so many possibilities for us, I can't even name them all. It's the future, Jimmy. We can go anywhere now. And… you can be part of that, if you want in?'

'A job?' asked James, his expression brightening. 'Not just a one-time deal. You're offering me a job?'

'It's yours if you want it, my man. "Commander James Fowler, captain of the *Aurora*." Has a nice ring, don't it?'

James opened and closed his mouth stupidly. He'd only ever considered his flight in the *Aurora* as a one-and-done. Test the drive, report the findings, and go back to Chigwell with Angela. But this offer was too good to pass up. The test flight had highlighted there were significant risks, but the danger didn't bother him. He was hooked. There was now no question in his mind about the decision he should make. But would Angela be okay with it? He'd already put her through hell just on this one trip, and he hadn't had a good track record with space missions so far.

He looked at her. 'How do you feel about it?

Angela sat up and played with the sleeve of his t-shirt. 'I think you're fucking insane, but you're the immortal.'

She squeezed James's arm gently, the weight of the world seemed on her shoulders. 'I'm the one that pushed you into this because I saw you were miserable. I can't keep you from it. I couldn't live with myself if I took away your chance to be who you are again.'

'But I should be there for you.'

'Oh, you'd better!'

James snorted. 'Fair enough. But, are you really okay with this?'

'For fuck's sake, of course I am. I wouldn't be saying it otherwise, you div! It's where you belong.'

James nodded, then leaned over and kissed her. Without a further word, he stood and reached over to Austin with his hand outstretched.

'You've got yourself a deal, Captain.'

The Augment Saga continues in:
Newton's Reach & The Shadow of Arcadia

ABOUT THE AUTHOR

Alan K. Dell is a British sci-fi author and creative person with far too many hobbies. He writes science fiction described as 'by, and for, sci-fi geeks' and loves to explore interesting high-tech concepts in his work. Outside of writing, he is a book blogger and reviewer, avid videogamer, archer, photographer, and musician. For his day job he works as Parish Administrator for his local church. He lives at home in Essex with his wife and two children.

Get in touch (he doesn't bite!):
Website: www.alankdell.co.uk
Social Media: bio.site/alankdell
Goodreads: www.goodreads.com/alankdell

Please take the time to leave a review on Amazon or Goodreads. It would be greatly appreciated and it's a brilliant way to support authors.

MORE IN THE AUGMENT SAGA

THE RE-EMERGENCE
An Augment Saga Novella

FROM THE GRAVE OF THE GODS
The Augment Saga: Book One

༄

NEWTON'S REACH
An Augment Saga Short Story

THE SHADOW OF ARCADIA
The Augment Saga: Book Two

LEGACY OF THE GODS
The Augment Saga: Book Three

OTHER BOOKS BY THE AUTHOR

THE GOD SUN
A Cosmic Horror Sci-Fi Novelette

www.ingramcontent.com/pod-product-compliance
Lightning Source LLC
LaVergne TN
LVHW030242250326
834688LV00047B/1765